THE EXISTENTIAL DETECTIVE

Alice Thompson

TWO RAVENS
P R E S S

Published by Two Ravens Press Ltd.
Green Willow Croft
Rhiroy, Lochbroom
Ullapool, IV23 2SF
United Kingdom

www.tworavenspress.com

ISBN: 978-1-906120-51-1

British Library Cataloguing in Publication Data: a CIP record for this book can be obtained from the British Library.

Designed and typeset in Sabon by Two Ravens Press;
cover design by Two Ravens Press.

Cover art: The Mystery and Melancholy of a Street, 1914
(oil on canvas) by Giorgio de Chirico (1888-1978).
Private collection | The Bridgeman Art Library.
© DACS 2009

Printed in Poland on Forest Stewardship
Council-accredited paper.

The publisher gratefully acknowledges subsidy from
the Scottish Arts Council towards the publication of this volume.

Scottish
Arts Council

About the Author

Alice Thompson was born and brought up in Edinburgh. She was the keyboard player with post-punk eighties band, The Woodentops and joint winner with Graham Swift of The James Tait Black Memorial Prize for Fiction for her first novel, *Justine*. Her second novel, *Pandora's Box*, was shortlisted for The Stakis Prize for Scottish Writer of the Year. Her other novels are *Pharos*, and most recently *The Falconer* (Two Ravens Press, 2008). Alice is a past winner of a Creative Scotland Award. She lives in Edinburgh.

For more information about the author, see

www.tworavenspress.com

Acknowledgements

Thanks to Sharon Blackie and David Knowles, Jenny Brown, Aidan and Charlotte Day, Alan and Mary Thompson, Hamish Thompson, Heather Pulliam and Whitney McVeigh.

The author is grateful to Warner/Chappell Music Ltd for permission to reprint lyrics from Pat Ballard's *Mister Sandman*.

All characters in this work are fictitious. Any resemblance to real persons, living or dead, is purely coincidental.

To Stephen and Isaac

Mister Sandman, bring me a dream
Make him the cutest that I've ever seen
Give him two lips like roses and clover
Then tell him that his lonesome nights are over

Sandman, I'm so alone
Don't have nobody to call my own
Please turn on your magic beam
Mister Sandman, bring me a dream

Mister Sandman
PAT BALLARD

The image of the cruel sandman now assumed hideous detail within me, and when I heard the sound of clumping coming up the stairs in the evening I trembled with fear and terror. My mother could get nothing out of me but the cry 'The sandman! the sandman!' stammered out in tears. I was the first to run into the bedroom on the nights he was coming, and his fearsome apparition tormented me till dawn. I was already old enough to realize that the tale the old woman had told me of the children's nest in the moon could not be true; nevertheless, the sandman himself remained a dreadful spectre; and I was seized with especial horror whenever I heard him not merely come up the stairs but wrench open the door of my father's study and go into it. There were times when he stayed away for many nights; then he would come all the more frequently, night after night.

The Sandman
E.T.A. HOFFMANN

Chapter 1

Portobello was a place where you could find anonymity, and Will enjoyed the faded seaside resort's genteel seediness because it demanded nothing from him. The pale deserted promenade that ran along the edge of the flat sea, the mishmash of small Georgian cottages and red stone tenements and the amusement arcade seemed to represent to Will his own pleasurable disillusionment. Of medium height, he appeared inconspicuous – he liked to blend into whatever landscape he was walking into and his ashen skin made him look as if he slept under rocks. Dark curly hair overshadowed a strong face which was slightly concave but detachedly handsome, as if the world had given him a few punches over the years and then stepped back to admire its handiwork.

It was a typical autumn day as Will walked along the promenade. The seagulls were as clamorous as ever. The rain of the night before had been heavy and he could hear the water rushing down the huge pipe that ran beneath the promenade and led directly into the sea. There was no wind. The sea was still. He loved the windless days.

Shrugging off his raincoat, Will climbed the stairs to the small office, above the fish-and-chip café, where he worked and lived. The sign on the door read *William Blake, Private Investigator.* Over time it made him smile, for he investigated the most secret and sordid matters, generally involving infidelity or fraud, until the word *private* had become blurred with his knowledge of other peoples' lives.

He quickly glanced around the room to check nothing had been disturbed. A few days earlier he had been broken into. A few papers had been rearranged and some old family photos he hadn't looked at in years had been scattered across the floor, but nothing had been taken as far as he could see. In fact, something had been added: he had found the packaging of a disposable camera in his wastepaper bin.

Today was a boring day. A few phone calls about forged cheques, filial deception and a missing cat. That evening, he retired to his living room which lay at the back of the flat and looked not over the sea but over another row of tenement blocks behind. He always entered it with a sense of relief; it was a sanctuary from the chaos.

He bent down to pick up a parcel just behind the door that had been hand-delivered that morning; only his name was typed on the front. He shook it. Bits inside rattled. He tore off the brown paper – inside there was a box with no accompanying note or letter.

He opened it up to find a jigsaw. It must have been sent by someone who knew he liked puzzles. The pieces inside were tiny; it looked fiendishly difficult, he noted with delight. They were mostly greys and flesh tones with the odd flash of colour. Will stared at it until he grew so tired he leant his head on the table and fell asleep. He woke up after midnight, his head aching, and collapsed into bed without bothering to undress.

The next morning it was raining again, but even harder. It rained so hard as he worked at his desk that it seemed as if his thoughts had turned to a relentless patter of water on stone. Outside his window, the sky and sea merged in a seamless grey. The seagulls were fighting for sodden bread left on the sand by the little Chinese girl, Lily. She generally fed them old fish from the café below every morning. He could hear the gulls squabbling. It annoyed him, the way she kept feeding them. The birds' noise was such a distraction, but he couldn't be bothered to ask her to stop.

There was a knock on the open door of his office. Will looked up. Standing in the doorway was a tall man wearing a shabby brown corduroy suit. He slumped down in the chair opposite Will's desk, gazing at him with benign, appraising eyes.

It was faces that Will liked to read most. Faces that told their stories. He could read lives in their lines, the shape of their jaw. Youth was a good disguise: its puppy fat and smooth skin were like blank pages. But age, yes; age marked people.

Will, on the other hand, like to keep his own face impassive. He knew one of the rules of detecting, one of the cardinal rules, was not to be read first. Preferably not to be read at all. For the detective was not part of the story but the outsider looking in: the reader, not the book. Will was there to solve cases – if his presence affected events, clues would be disturbed, ripples made in the water.

The client took from his pocket a small photograph and laid it on his desk. Will looked down at the photo. It was a picture of a young woman, about twenty years old. She had an extremely smooth, moulded face, like a mask, with a straightly chiselled nose and almond-shaped dark eyes.

'I'd like you to find my wife.'

Of course she was his wife, Will thought. This client would

have been the sort of man attracted to an immutable girl like that. He had an almost feminine face and large green eyes that made Will think he must operate in instinctive, clever ways. His presence was dynamic: not dominating or overbearing but closed-off and intense, as if all his thoughts had trapped his emotions within him and they were now clamouring inside like small wild birds. Why had he at first thought the client was her father? He judged his client to be about forty years old, old enough to be her father.

'You've lost her?'

'Four days ago. I came back home from work and she'd gone.'

'She's normally at home waiting for you?'

He shrugged his shoulders noncommittally. 'And you haven't seen her since?'

'No.'

'And you are?'

'Adam Verver. Dr Adam Verver.'

'When was this photo taken?'

'About a year ago.' He had a quiet voice. 'She still looks the same.'

Verver paused, about to say something, and Will waited for him to continue. He was good at hearing the rhythm and patterns of conversation, the tiny heartbeats of silence.

'She suffers from amnesia,' Adam finally said.

He seemed reluctant to elucidate. Will knew better than to go further than a client wanted on a first meeting. His job was not only to solve a case, it was to let the client see that he could be trusted. That way, he could generally get more information in the end. This man was the touchstone to the solution. The one closest to the disappeared generally was.

4

'I see. But she knows who she is?'

'She can remember everything of the past four years. But no memories before then.'

Will tried a different tack.

'What about a friend she may have visited?'

'She didn't have friends.' Dr Verver managed to make "friends" sound like the name of an infectious disease.

'Who was the last to see her?'

'My parents, Lord and Lady Verver. And their staff.' Dr Verver spoke of his parents very neutrally. Will couldn't detect any antagonism.

'And you haven't contacted the police?'

'I'd rather not. It's a personal matter.'

'I understand. I'll need to question everyone in the house.'

Dr Verver gave him the address of his parents.

'I'll come round this afternoon.'

'I'll let my father know.'

'I will also search your wife's room. And look around your house.'

'Of course. It's not a house, actually. It's a flat.'

'Do you and your wife live there alone?'

He was careful to use the present tense; not to put her in the past tense. Adam nodded.

'And your work is?'

'I'm a scientist.'

'Ah.' It explained a kind of subtle arrogance about him. Will couldn't resist looking at his client's hands, long fine fingers. This man in front of him, he thought, was only interested in what Will could do for him. But for money, so Will didn't mind that.

'I work long hours. It's my life.'

Will nodded. He knew what he meant.

Will belonged to the Association of Private Investigators. A lot of his cases involved marital betrayal, which involved working night and day. He spent a lot of time examining theatre tickets and drink receipts. Infidelity meant business to him. It was usually married women who came to him. If only women knew, he thought, what infidelity meant to some men. How little it meant anything.

He had learnt never to get involved in a case, to always remain one step removed. On the whole he was helping the victims. It was the betrayers, those who deceived, that he traced. He was once told by a jealous wife that she would like to take out a contract on her husband's mistress. He said no. Will believed in unconventional justice but he drew the line at contract killing.

Technology hadn't made much of a difference to detecting. Nothing in the end could replace the efficacy of following someone. Following the traces, standing in doorways, looking at what was behind you in the reflection of shop windows. Following someone who did not know they were being followed, didn't even know of his existence.

Chapter 2

Lily was feeding seagulls again on the beach. The seagulls fluttered violently around her, above her head. Her oriental face was still and placid, as if her emotions had flown into the birds around her.

'Hi, Lily,' he said.

She turned round and looked at him. She never smiled. Always gave him the same serious look of recognition when she saw his face.

'You don't think you may be overfeeding them? They're beginning to look a bit fat.'

'You just don't like me feeding them.'

'What's wrong with them catching fish?'

'It's hard for them to get the flies on the hooks.'

'Lily, facetiousness isn't attractive.'

'Well, then you should try something else.' She then turned to feeding the gulls again.

They were a close family in the fish-and-chip shop. Extended family with that detached sense of happiness only real intimacy can bring and Will looked upon it with fear. The Chinese family chattered amongst themselves but mostly he would see them working hard in the café. He often saw Lily cleaning the tables and sweeping the floor after school, the smell of the frying fish accompanying her out into the sea air.

At the east end of the Promenade was a row of Gothic

houses. With their turrets and towers they reminded Will of a stage set out of *A Hammer House of Horror*. Designed in the mid-nineteenth century, they had been built originally for rich merchants who wanted to show off their wealth. The gardens were larger and set further back from the promenade than the other houses and clearly still had monied owners.

The garden of Lord and Lady Verver was fronted by a large wall and an iron gate, shutting it off from the rest of the world. Stuck on a lamppost outside their house was a 'missing person' poster for Louise Verver – in mint condition, it reminded Will of a poster for a missing cat. Above her picture were the words:

MISSING
Louise Verver
5'4". Dark brown eyes, brunette, medium build
Suffers from amnesia

He looked at her face again. The expression in her eyes had a quality he couldn't fathom. It wasn't sadness, he thought, nor was it fear. He flickered over her long brown hair, her cheekbones, her narrow nose. He realized, as he took a step back, looking at the whole face, what it was. It was a lack of any emotion at all; it was an absence of character.

He went up the path and rang the doorbell. He waited a while before the housekeeper opened the door. She was an unfriendly looking woman with short greying hair and an unmade-up face. She tried to smile.

'Good afternoon. I'm William Blake.' He showed her his card. 'I've come to ask Lord Verver about the disappearance of his daughter-in-law.'

The housekeeper's fixed smile at once vanished.

'Ah yes, of course. It's all worrying. Very worrying. Come in. I'm Mrs Elliot. They call me Mary.'

She ushered him into the grand entrance hall. His footsteps echoed on the black and white tiles. For a moment, the housekeeper scuttled about rearranging letters on a side-table. He noticed her distracted manner. As duplicity was part of his work, it made it easy for him to recognize it in others.

A moose's head hung above a heavy stone fireplace that was carved with gargoyles, and a large staircase wound its way up to the first floor. There was money in the Ververs' house. The painting, the Persian carpets, the thin coldness of the air, all whispered wealth.

The atmosphere was not ostentatious, just pervasive. But strangely, there was also a faded careworn feel to the house: the carpets were threadbare. A powerful smell of lilies from the hall table mingled with a smell of must, reminding him of a funeral parlour.

'Your staircase bannisters are looking very shiny, Mary,' Will said.

As she turned to admire them herself, Will quickly glanced down at the side-table where she had slipped a letter under a pile of documents as he had come into the hall. He pulled it our from under the pile.

It was a half-opened brown envelope addressed in clumsy misspelling to Adam Verver. The edges of some photographs were peeping out. He wondered if Mary had taken a surreptitious look at them and was now protecting the son of her employer.

'What did you think of Louise?' he asked as she turned around again.

'Oh, a very nice lady,' but her lower lip went down slightly, in a kind of grimace.

On the first floor she crossed the landing to a large oak door and opened it. Will entered a large living room and Mary quietly shut the door behind him. The view of the sea was breathtaking, stretching out to an empty horizon. Because of the perspective, the promenade and beach were out of view – it was as if the house was protruding out of the sea.

'Hallo, Mr Blake. You're the detective who's come about Adam's disappearing wife, I suppose. My son told me to expect a visit from you.'

The large booming voice startled Will: a resonant, centuries-old voice, as if pulled tightly over Stradivarius wood. In one of the dark corners of the room sat an old man in a wheelchair, his legs covered by a tweed blanket.

As he wheeled himself slowly and deliberately out of the shadows into the light, his shrunken persona contrasted with his deep dominant voice. His voice was far larger than the real man, reminding Will of the wizard of Oz. The rug slipped off to reveal two withered and lifeless legs and William bent down and placed the rug back over him.

'That's very kind of you, young man. If you ask me, she's just wandered off. Forgotten where she is. Someone will find her and bring her back in, I'm sure.'

He sounded as if he were talking about a stray dog, William thought: one without a pedigree.

'Has she done this before? Wandered off like this?'

'Women nowadays are a dissatisfied lot. Always bemoaning their fate. My wife is just the same. As if we all didn't have a fate to bemoan.'

He looked down at his legs.

His face still was handsome, in spite of the drawn skin – ancient and wrinkled like parchment written over many times in ink. He looked chivalrous. He had a strong jawline and high forehead that made him seem incisive, analytical, not prone to emotion or self-knowledge. Hardly sexual now, but once would have been, very. But there was also something about his face that was self-centred, a sense that things were his due.

'So she has gone missing before?'

Lord Verver hesitated. He took out a cigarette from a silver lighter case and lit it. He inhaled, all the while keeping his gaze on Will. He had a piercing glare. He was under no illusions, Will thought. He knew all about human nature, what men and women were like.

'How can I put this tactfully, Mr Blake?'

'In my line of work, Lord Verver, tact just tends to delay things.'

'Indeed. Indeed. A few months ago she started going down to the amusement arcade. Hours she would spend there. To play on those damned machines.' He smiled dryly. 'She seems to have an affinity with them.'

'She likes to gamble?'

Lord Verver snorted. 'It seems so.'

So what kind of person did Louise Verver's gambling make her? Someone who wanted to escape from reality. Someone who liked to think they could control the outcome of their gambling. Gamblers didn't believe in luck. They believed in the power of mind over matter.

'Did Adam argue with her? Try to stop her?'

Adam's father wheeled his wheelchair into the adjacent conservatory, picked up a watering can, and began to water the tomatoes.

'Of course. Isn't that what the spouses of gamblers do? It becomes a way of life to try and stop them.'

'But it never got violent?'

'Of course not. I never saw him raise a finger to her. Or heard anything to that effect.'

'You never saw her with a black eye? Anything of that kind?'

'No.' He held Will's gaze.

The Ververs were very wealthy, he thought. They had a sense of privilege that was ingrained in their character. He wondered what Adam thought of his wife haunting the amusement arcade.

As if reading his mind, Lord Verver said quickly, 'Adam indulges her. Will do anything for her. Besotted by her. The kind of infatuation that certain intense men hold for their wives, that excludes everything else.'

Why was Will getting the impression that Lord Verver was lying?

'When would she gamble?'

'Any time, day or night. Very odd girl.' There was latent anger in his voice now. It was the first time he had showed emotion. In Will's line of work anger was often the first emotion you saw in people. Anger seemed to be the default emotion. People fell into it, as if the other emotions were too much hard work, but anger was a walk in the park.

'She had amnesia when Adam met her?'

'Yes. He brought her into our lives like a magician pulling a rabbit out of a hat. She was a young rabbit at that – just sixteen. He seemed to conjure her up out of the air. No memories at all as far as I could tell. But she was eager to please, in full possession of her faculties and all that. Ironically, recently she seemed to be getting some memories back.'

Will wondered if "ironically" was the right word. Perhaps there was a connection between her memory coming back and her disappearance.

'Her childhood memories?' he asked.

'Yes. Just in the weeks that led up to her going missing. She was becoming very confused.'

'Well, thank you, Lord Verver. You've been very helpful.'

'Glad to have been of help. Puzzling case. Most puzzling. You must understand, my Adam is a very unusual person. Just because he's eccentric doesn't mean he's violent. He may be erratic and so on. That's why people tend to misunderstand him. They get the wrong end of the stick. You know the kind of thing, I'm sure.'

'I do. For some people the wrong end of the stick can be like a magnet.'

Lord Verver gave a chuckle. 'I'm glad you understand.'

He wheeled himself vigorously forward and shook Will's hands. As Will was leaving the conservatory, he turned round to see Lord Verver picking some dead leaves off the tomatoes. He looked pale and anxious. The stern autocratic face had become vulnerable and frightened. And Will guessed it probably didn't have anything to do with the mildew on the Little Napoleon fruit.

William left the house. The father and son were an odd pair. One bluffly masculine, in spite of paralysis, the other introverted but passionate. And this strange missing woman at the centre of the case, connecting the father reluctantly with his son. Will wondered if the real tension was not between

Louise and her father-in-law, but between father and son. Louise fulfilled a useful function, as scapegoats often did in a family. They made everyone else in the family feel normal. He still felt that he didn't really have an idea what she was like. Her behaviour, yes, but not how she was.

William walked back down the promenade to his flat. Unlocking his door, he felt relief as he always did when entering his private world. Pouring himself a Talisker, he sat down to begin the jigsaw. He was methodical in a way he wasn't with his cases, beginning at the sides, collecting all the darker pieces first. This was going to take a long time, he thought, as he began the lower edge – but he would get there in the end.

Chapter 3

The next morning, Will visited the amusement arcade on the promenade. It seemed so ludicrously out of place amongst the grey old stones of the town. The arcade was both an illusion and the face of hard cash, its slot machines tinny and bright and brash and motored by the fantasies of man. Outside, the dark rain fell on the potholes of the promenade; inside, coloured light flickered amongst the maelstrom of cymbals and melodies. The flashing of fruit machines shone out from the interior darkness like neon fish in a gloomy aquarium. The arcade whispered riches and wealth amongst the piles of old and tired coins on the sliding machines. A place of money, in this poor seaside resort the arcade promised dreams.

A gaudily painted mural ran above the entrance of the arcade. It depicted a young man holding a sword, its blade dripping with blood, standing beside a flame-haired girl. Both figures were looking down pitilessly at a dying woman, lying at their feet. It was a scene from the Greek myth of Elektra, in which she persuades her brother Orestes to kill her mother in revenge for the death of her father. Running above the mural, written in fake gothic lettering, were the words *Et in arcadia ego*.

The arcade held a certain fascination, Will could see that. It was only the huge twenty-foot statue of a plastic clown laughing through the window that gave it away. The clown's oppressive dark red and green tones gave the figure a lugubrious, sinister quality. The smiling insane face was the front of money and greed. Ostensibly, the clown was to lure children in, like the child catcher of *Chitty Chitty Bang Bang* with his lollipops. But in reality it was a giant toy for the grown-up children.

A few truanting boys in their early teens were hanging about on bikes outside the amusement arcade. They had the faces of forty-year-olds on lean stricken bodies, as if they had snatched at their futures too soon. Will wondered if they were dealing drugs. They had both energy and amorality, like indiscriminate gods. But there was one fair-haired boy whose impassivity set him apart from the others.

Will could hear the familiar music pounding away from inside the arcade – it was Abba's *Money, Money, Money,* and he entered feeling as if he were descending into Dante's inferno.

An old woman sat at one slot machine, a middle-aged man in a dark blue worn suit stood at another, his eyes filled with fire as he played it. This amusement arcade, Will thought, with its gaudy lights, its raucous noise, was what people mistook for entertainment. When really, as they pulled down the levers of the slot machines, they were ratcheting away their despair.

After his divorce Will had given everything to his wife: the house in Portobello, the savings. He didn't want anything any more. It clouded what he needed to know. He didn't know what it was he needed to know; he only knew that money, possessions weren't a part of any knowledge he wanted a share in.

'Can I help you?' Will was shaken out of his reverie by a young man coming towards him wearing beige trousers, tight black shirt and – in spite of being indoors – a trilby on the back of his head. He looked like a dancer when he walked and moved, as if he was used to setting the pace. He had a very sensual, fleshed-out face with a bald head and dark liquid brown eyes. A very strong personality, Will thought; he was a voluptuous thing. Emblazoned incongruously on the front of his black shirt was Oedipus wearing one sandal, presumably to echo the mythic scene depicted above the outside entrance.

The man stretched out his hand to Will.

'Mikael,' he said, in a thick Russian accent.

Will introduced himself as a detective; Mikael didn't flinch.

Will showed him the picture of Louise Verver. 'Do you recognize her?'

Again, Mikael showed no sign of concern or guilt. 'That would be Louise. Her father-in-law owns the arcade. She's a regular customer. Comes in most days.'

His voice sounded neutral, too neutral. He knows something, Will thought, he was sure of it. Is he in contact with her? Will also wondered why Lord Verver hadn't told him of his business interests in the arcade.

'Can you say when you last saw her?'

He paused. 'Now you come to mention it, I haven't seen her for a few days or so. She was in nearly every day.'

A teenage Goth was walking by, her black hair scraped back, her face powdered white. Will wondered what she would look like without make-up. A scared schoolgirl, he thought. A vague headache was starting up at the back of his head – the music and the lights weren't helping.

'You're asking about Louise?' Her voice was surprisingly

gentle.

'The detective's asking when we last saw her.'

'It was last week. I remember it well 'cos she was acting strangely.'

'How?'

'As she was playing the machines, she kept muttering to herself. She'd never said anything much before … just did the machines.'

'Muttering what?'

'Something like, "They're coming back, they're coming back" … and then suddenly she rushed out … Actually,' the girl remembered, 'she left something here. Her bag.'

Will felt the familiar excitement of a sudden, unexpected clue. 'Have you still got it?'

'I put it behind the desk. I've been meaning to contact her, but forgot.'

She went and collected the bag. Will emptied it out onto the desk. Just a few pennies, a lipstick, and an address book. He picked up the address book. To his surprise, flicking through the names, he saw *William Blake* and his own address written down. She must have made a note of it while passing his office on the promenade. However, to see his name in this missing woman's address book disturbed him. He didn't want to be a part of anyone's life, let alone part of the disappearing case he was working on. It was a coincidence he didn't like.

Will disliked coincidences. His work was full of them and it was difficult to separate coincidence from motive and intention. Coincidences confused matters. A coincidence could imprison an innocent man who was in the wrong place at the wrong time, could rob people of their children.

Coming out of the arcade he saw the gang of boys still there on their bikes, talking to Mikael. But it was the fair-haired boy's hand that Mikael shook. At the same time, Will saw him slip a package into the boy's hand, a barely perceptible, practical movement with the kick of an illegal transaction. Will thought it must have been drugs. It often came down to drugs in the end. It was just that the package seemed too big for a general handover – the size of a paperback book. Bigger deals never took place in public places. Hotel rooms, empty warehouses, garages – but not outside.

~

That evening, after eating, Will felt restless and decided to visit Granny's Attic, a drinking den on the promenade he sometimes frequented. It was on the first floor of a Victorian tenement block. He climbed up the gloomy steps into a wooden-floored room with subdued lighting and basic wooden chairs and tables. The smell of alcohol and sweat merged with the trace of over-sweet perfume.

One or two men nursed drinks at the side-tables, their faces unrecognizable in the gloom. When the lights illuminated their faces they looked old and scared. A waitress with dyed blonde hair, mouse-like features and a buxom body who had been standing by the small bar came over to him and took his order. She brought a small whisky to him. Then she hovered.

'Here on your own?' she asked in a husky voice, her brash blonde hair at odds with her small-featured face.

Will sipped the whisky, savouring the acrid taste. 'It's the only way to be,' he said.

She laughed. 'Oh, come on, no one likes to be on their own. Everyone needs a little company now and then.' She reached out and touched his hand and looked straight into his eyes. He was surprised by the look in her pale blue gaze, a loving maternal look, full of affection.

'What's your name?'

'Nancy.'

'Well, Nancy, let me tell you this. I've been on my own for many years. I've got used to it. It suits me.'

Nancy appeared visibly taken aback by his cold tone.

'And shall I tell you why?' he continued. 'Because human company smells of old food in a fridge. That, Nancy, is why I like to be on my own. Now how much is the whisky?'

'£2.75.'

Giving her three pounds, he told her, 'Keep the change.'

Slowly and deliberately she extracted some coins from the leather pouch around her waist and counted out 25p.

'You keep the change. You look like you need it,' she said. She let the coins drop one by one with a clatter on the table next to his drink and walked away on her high heels.

Will took another sip of the peaty liquid. A middle-aged couple sat down opposite him. They sat close together with the hunted euphoric look of the unfaithful, as if a romantic song was constantly playing inside their heads as background music to whatever they did. Will looked at them pityingly. He liked to do pity; it made him feel better. Nancy came and went as she took their order, studiously ignoring Will.

Neon spotlights switched on above the stage floor and coloured lights of bright yellow, green and red started to encircle the floor. A jazz version of *Mister Sandman* came on through the amplifiers. A singer would be due on soon – the music a signal that the show was soon to begin.

Will took a gulp of his whisky. The previous squalor and

general emptiness of the room, now seen through the veil of drink and flashing lights and music, were taking on a fuzzy attractive glow. What was he wanting from all this, he wondered, the whisky burning his throat.

Time passed and Will became lost in a maze of memories, images of the past flickering across his vision. Then the singer walked onto the stage. She was wearing a sleeveless, platinum evening dress, the sequins shining a pattern of rainbow lights. It was as if she were made of metal, he thought, metal wrought from the hard resilience of her youth.

As she started swaying to the music, she began to sing

Mister Sandman, bring me a dream
Make him the cutest I've ever seen
Give him two lips like roses and clover
Then tell him that his lonesome nights are over

whilst outside the sea and wind howled. A peroxide blonde, the singer had eyes so blue – a vivid, unreal blue – that they made his heart miss a beat. But above all, the youth of her – the soft luminous skin, the limpid eyes, the slender arms. He was halfway to death and now this young woman had walked into his life out of the blue. He had come across her.

And for a moment her hard platinum look seemed to dissolve into the neon light of the disco, her body fragmenting into atoms of colour, becoming a diffuse swaying of light. Her voice had become the only substantial thing about her as her body dissolved into its strong melody.

However, as Will continued to stare, he saw a hardening in the lapidary eyes, noticed the lips darkening – until they became the colour of blood. Her body was swaying to the solitary music of her own introverted desire. And his heart sank – what had he been thinking of – a moment of hallucinatory, impossible longing.

Having finished her song, the singer quickly left the stage and Will decided to return home. As he walked down the corridor out of Granny's Attic, he noticed the same fair-haired boy he had seen outside the arcade walking towards him. Will was not particularly surprised; arbitrariness had become his god, a chimerical god that constantly changed its shape. And Portobello was a small place.

As the boy was wearing his i-Pod, he seemed oblivious to the detective. Will could hear the tinny sound of electro music leaking from the ear-pieces. Will ducked into the darkness, then followed the boy backstage to the dressing room.

The boy knocked on the door and handed over to the singer the package that Mikael had slipped him. Will wondered again what was in the package. Drugs were a failure of the imagination, a catastrophic destruction of dreams. Sure, drugs had their own fantasy, but it was not your own. It was a collective imagination that left the individual's dreams undreamt. It was like paying for someone else to dream for you. But the singer didn't strike him as someone who wanted anyone else's dreams but Mister Sandman's.

Chapter 4

The next morning seven swans floated in the sea along the edge of the shore. Will was reminded of the fairy story about the seven princes who were turned into swans and the princess who sewed them shirts out of stinging nettles with her bare hands to try to turn them back into princes.

People stared at the unusual sight. It was not usual to see swans in the sea. Necks high and regal, wings carefully folded, they looked as if they were on a mission: a mission to be watched and admired. They dominated even the sea, those seven big white birds.

It was a washed-clean morning after the huge downpour of the day before. The puddles reflected the sky and water had filled the cracks in the concrete of the promenade. Soaked by the rain, the dense and spongy sand had turned orange. The 'missing person' poster of Louise was peeling off the lamppost. Peeping out from underneath was another poster of a missing person. Will peeled away Louise's picture to reveal the photo of a young girl with black hair and an impish face. *Jade* was scrawled beneath the photo in illiterate handwriting. The poster was dog-eared and fraying at the edges. Will felt he had seen the writing before. He smoothed the newer poster back down over the older one.

Then a flash of red – conspicuous against the beige sand – caught his eye. A woman, wearing a dress the colour of blood, was approaching the swans. It was the direct line of her walk that seemed so odd. People on the beach generally meandered. She was unwavering. It was as if she were going to walk straight into the sea. All his instinct as a private investigator convinced him that this woman – at this time, in this place, above all with him watching – was without doubt Louise Verver.

He leapt over the small wall that separated the promenade from the beach and ran across the damp thick sand toward the woman and the swans. The tide was low and she was about a hundred yards below him, approaching the water's edge. She still didn't turn around. Something made Will pause. He wanted to see if she would walk into the water – it looked as if that was what was going to happen. He was curious about her state of mind. It was as if these swans were something to do with her lost memories.

As he watched her looking at the swans, a strong feeling overcame him. A surfeit of some ineffable emotion rose up in him. And he watched as the swans unfolded their wings, raised up their bodies high and engulfed her – she didn't scream or resist. Her body disappeared between the vigorous beating of their white-feathered wings.

He caught his breath, his throat constricting, and fell down onto the sand. The last thing he felt before losing consciousness was his face imprinting itself on the damp, solid beach.

A while later, he turned his head and looked up to see Lily looking down at him implacably.

'Are you okay?'

Will staggered to his feet. He looked down the beach. The woman had gone. The swans had swum a few hundred yards further down the shore. He looked down at himself. His jeans and jumper were covered in sand. He spit sand out of his mouth. Lily smiled. It was the first time he had seen her smile.

'You look like a sandman,' she said.

Solemnly, she held out a tissue and he wiped the sand from his face.

'Did you see what happened?'

'You were looking at the swans. Then you dropped down onto the sand.'

'Did you see what happened to the woman who walked into the water?'

'I didn't see a woman. Just the swans.' Lily looked at him with dark eyes.

'Brunette, slim, in her twenties,' he insisted.

Lily shook her head. 'There were just the swans.' Like the first line of a haiku.

Will gave up, it didn't matter. He shivered, he always felt cold after one of his visions. He also felt thirsty. Lily took him back to the café and brought him a cup of hot tea.

'Are you okay now?'

He smiled. 'Be careful. You're sounding like you care.'

She looked at him crossly. 'You and your imagination!'

He returned home and put on some jazz. The room was pleasantly dark and gloomy.

When the fits had started a couple of years ago, he had delayed going to the doctor. After suffering a few seizures, William had begun to think of the fits – and the visions that came with them – as indistinguishable from his memories, imagination and thought; they all seemed confused in the brain's neural network. In his mind the real and fantastical had become the same. Weren't memories, after all, just rewritten stories, various versions of the real? Wasn't everyone just carrying around stories in their heads?

But after a year, the seizures had become so intense that Will decided to ask for medical help. The neurologist could give no physical reason for why the convulsions had started, other than severe mental trauma. He was given antipsychotic drugs. The drugs dulled his senses and thoughts, which initially was a relief; he walked through life as if walking underwater. Everything seemed to be submerged, everything slowed down – but he knew his work was suffering. And he needed his work. So he came off the drugs. The visions came back as frequently and intensely as before and he grew to live with them as if they were waking dreams.

The next morning he noticed the flashing red light of his answer phone – one message, from Adam Verver.

'I need to see you.'

An hour later Adam was putting down a heap of red material on Will's desk.

'I found this on the beach.'

Will looked at the torn dress. It looked like the same dress he had seen Louise wear on the beach the day before. The dress had been cut into pieces, like a material jigsaw. Will picked up the pieces carefully; there were no traces of blood, or any other sign of violence, just the cut silk, sinister in itself.

In Will's experience, the less he told clients the better. If he expressed ideas or possibilities, they invariably latched onto the one they wanted to believe in. And this would distort what they knew or believed from then on. He could get a clearer picture of the truth if the clients remained in the dark for longer. Will specialized in ambiguity; he himself had constantly to live with it until the truth variously suggested itself to him.

He was beginning to feel this case was different from his previous ones. There was something more personal and intimate about it; it disturbed him.

'Perhaps we should bring in the police,' Will advised reluctantly.

Adam went pale. His wide-apart eyes focused on the detective piercingly, as if willing him out of the suggestion.

'No, I don't want that,' Adam said.

'They'll be able to help in ways I can't.'

'No, I don't want the police involved. It's a matter of privacy. I know we can sort it out ourselves.'

He doesn't want the police any more than I do, thought Will. He looked at the cut-up fabric again – it seemed like the work of a psychopath. Either that, or Louise in a state of confusion had cut up the dress herself.

Will returned to the arcade at closing time and hung around the doorway. Detectives and criminals, he thought, how could you tell them apart just by looking? Coming out, Mikael was easily recognizable, in spite of the dark rainy day, by his broad shoulders and rhythmic way of walking. The attendant walked as if he were glancing off the space around him. Will followed him down the promenade to Granny's Attic. He climbed up the steps to the bar and sat down at a table – Mikael was nowhere to be seen.

In the Attic it was slow and languid, the sporadic red flashing light only emphasising the slowness of the rest of the room. This was the fag-end of existence, the place where you waited. If the arcade was the inferno, this place was purgatory. And William never minded waiting. It made him feel irrationally as if he were cheating death. Death not as a mocking clown, the stuff of nightmares, but death as real as the sea that ebbed and flowed on the beach every day. There was a skill to waiting, he thought. Everyone should learn to wait. If people didn't wait, it would all be over before they knew it.

The frequency of the flashing red lights quickened and the music grew quieter as the singer came onto the stage. She was like an artefact, he thought. "Made-up" was the right phrase. Her sequinned aqua blue dress clung to her body like sea water hugging the contours of a coral beach. The blue of the dress matched the strong blue of her eyes. With her long blonde hair and the fishtail shape of her dress, she was like a mermaid. But not a natural mermaid: a toy Disney mermaid, exactingly perfect with full lips and yellow hair. She was not a mermaid who, having been given legs, would feel as if she were walking on knives. She was a mermaid out of a cartoon.

And then she began to sing again, huskily, slowly, and he could hear all of life in her voice. A vulnerability which didn't belong to the erotic mask of her visual persona. Like a ventriloquist's doll, it was as if she were speaking with someone else's voice. And this voice was also pulling him back, before he could stop himself, dragging him back into the past.

He was playing with Emily, his six-year-old daughter, playing tig in the dark woods of a fairy tale, where witches lived. Her smile was a row of perfectly formed seed-pearl teeth, the transaction of joy. As her father he felt his daughter's happiness, her life as his own, but then she disappeared into the dark shadows of the forest.

Will felt a strong sense of déjà vu as he followed the singer backstage after she had finished. Mikael was talking to her outside her stage door. Will quickly slipped behind the curtains. He was good at hiding. People picked up on emotions, auras, but if he watched without emotion, even without curiosity, he was invisible. He knew that as soon as he got too interested, felt too involved in a case, that would be when he would fall into danger. He would have become conspicuous.

He saw them talk, saw Mikael try to kiss her and then saw her resist. Mikael then put his burly arm around her and drew her into the shadows.

'What are you doing here?' he heard her whisper angrily.

'You know what I'm here for. You know I'd never let you down. Did the boy give you the package?'

She nodded.

'You had a chance to watch it.'

She nodded. The attendant was watching her, intensely focused.

'I should let you know there is a private detective nosing around. Hired by Adam. Looking for Louise.'

The singer smiled. 'Well, he'll never find her now, will he?'

Mikael turned round and Will quickly retreated out of Granny's Attic. He gulped the fresh cold sea air as if he had been gasping for breath and hadn't known it. Was Louise dead now, after all?

He had had his vision of her. But then Adam had found her cut-up dress on the beach soon afterwards. Had Louise been murdered soon after Will had seen her? Was she now lying under ten feet of heavy sand? Or had she been washed out to sea? The singer had sounded so final. But that voice. He had never heard anything so real. It was realer than the real world.

~

Portobello at night was at its most uncanny and quiet; the lamps leading down the promenade, the huge moon in the sky over the flat sea. Cold and still. It was like a photograph, he thought: a photograph not of the past but of the present. As Will walked down the promenade, he realized he preferred the darkness to unnatural light. The world, nature always told the truth. Men lied, made it bright when it was night, warm when it was cold. It was the truth Will was in love with. For the one incident in his life that had made him the man he was, or rather unmade him, the violent truth of what had happened in the past, was denied him.

Chapter 5

The swans were swimming up the small rivulet that led into the huge pipe that ran under the promenade. A few stood at the mouth of the pipe. Others swam, bending their heads gracefully to graze the water. They looked as if they were wondering what to do. They seemed unperturbed by a yapping dog that was running frantically up and down the beach. The swans turned and took off towards open sea, floating outwards as if making for the grey horizon.

A blind man with fair hair and fair skin, and open blue eyes that looked as if they could see, was taking his daily lunchtime walk. Will was struck by his innocent face. A woman would easily fall in love with him, he thought. That he couldn't see her would just make him more beautiful to her. Will rarely stopped to talk but this time the man's black labrador ran towards Will and leapt up at him. Will stroked its head and ears, the soft velvet head causing him a pang of joy.

'You hear a lot of things, I expect, round here,' he said to the blind man as he patted his dog.

'More than you would ever dream.'

'You didn't notice anything unusual about a week ago? A woman has gone missing from the promenade.'

The man's eyes flickered with his thoughts.

'Last week, I did hear something odd.'

'What was that?'

'I heard shouting.'

'From where?'

'Over there somewhere.' The blind man pointed to the new block of luxury flats. 'Where that scientist lives.'

'Who was shouting?'

'A woman. She was screaming out to the man, "You've lied to me. All these years. You've lied."'

Will watched the blind man's face carefully. It was still; the lips didn't waver or tremble, as happened in liars.

'And this was coming from inside the flat?'

'It seemed to be; it sounded a bit echoey. But she was shouting loudly.'

'Did she sound scared?'

The man paused, trying to think. 'No, not scared. Just angry and hurt.'

He would be expert, Will thought, at reading emotions in what he heard.

'So, she was talking to someone she knew well?'

'Oh, yes.'

'Like a lover's quarrel. Or an argument between husband and wife?'

'Exactly.'

It seemed that just before Louise went missing she had had an argument with her husband.

The blind man's dog was looking expectantly up at Will with wet dark eyes, and Will reached into his pocket and gave him a piece of old biscuit.

'You should get yourself a pet.'

'I'm a private investigator. I need to be quiet.'

'That figures. You know, you walk much more silently

than most people. Most people I can hear from twenty yards. You, I only hear when you've passed me.'

'That's good to know.'

'Well, if I pick up anything else about this missing woman, I'll tell you. People tend to be quite careless around me. Saying things they wouldn't normally do. Either they think because I'm blind I can't hear, or they like to make confessions.'

Will knew all about people's desire to confess. Sometimes he thought he was just there as a witness to deceit. But suspicious spouses went through the charade of employing him to watch the husband or wife cheat, just so that they could have a third person observe, to validate their feelings, like a psychologist. Make it real. Neither of them could admit the truth to each other. They needed a witness so they paid for him to discover what they already knew.

~

It is impossible to describe love for a child. He had wanted to protect Emily from the world, he had looked down at her in her crib and wanted to take the world from her.

As a toddler Emily would often be in bed by the time he got home. He would go into her room and see her lying there, pink from sleep, hot to touch, her little hand cupping her cheek in the same position she had held her hand in the womb. What sort of love was this, he thought, that had such fear of loss at its heart? What was beyond that loss was beyond imagining. He could not imagine the world without Emily; it was easier to imagine his own death.

As she grew older she thought of herself, as all children do, as immortal. Death was just an idea, a cartoon figure, a cut-out paper doll. He had secretly followed his six-year-old daughter making her first trip to see a friend around the corner, as if she were a mark. He had observed her excited hazel eyes glancing around, unable to believe the new world around her. Framed by a mass of red hair, a darker red than her mother's, her face was still unformed but a vitality shone out of every pore of her skin.

Emily had demanded his and Olivia's protection; it had been her most fundamental right. They had brought her into this unpredictable world and it had been their duty to look after her until she was ready to look after herself. And they had failed. And that failure was branded in his eyes and in the way Will walked. Will thought, here I am pursuing the guilty when really it is me I should be looking for, watching a while, before I find the final evidence of my guilt.

~

He had arranged to meet Olivia at the National Portrait Gallery in the centre of Edinburgh, where she worked as an art curator. It was a Gothic red building, full of intricate cornices and statues inserted into its exterior façade. The gallery was full of history, a different history from Portobello: the history of the establishment, the powerful and wealthy, the centre of the Enlightenment. Will found the gallery oppressive, as if the weight of history sucked the air out of his lungs. It was cold and dark inside. The portraits of people hung around the hall, all those faces looking down at him.

His ex-wife came out into the hall to greet him, as if she were one of the paintings come to life, gliding through the opulent cavernous rooms, the sound of her footsteps shifting from the soft pad of the carpet to the hard resonance of the wooden floors. She was dressed immaculately, her golden-red hair like the gilt frames of the portraits. When he had first set eyes on Olivia it was her physical differences from him that he had found so seductive. While he was heavy and sensual, she was delicate. She had a quick grace, a slim focused body that seemed so integral to who she was it had taken his breath away.

Seeing Olivia now was the only thing that could lift his spirits. She was wearing that enigmatic smile which seemed to defeat life. At the age of forty, she still had an unreadable face. This beguiled him. How much better an obscure text – how much more challenging, more erotic. Wasn't that an element of human desire, to work out, decipher, uncover, reveal?

There would always be something obscure about Olivia. He remembered noticing in the months before Emily's disappearance that Olivia had seemed more distant than usual. She had stayed at the gallery late; he could never get hold of her. Strangest of all was Olivia's lack of grief over Emily's disappearance. Outwardly, she seemed unperturbed. It would be like entering a town after a tornado had swept through it and seeing it untouched, people going about their business, litter still lying docilely in the street, children playing with paper aeroplanes. That was what Olivia was like, a town untouched. Functioning, business as usual, after the wind had torn through her.

'What are you thinking, William? You have that look on your face.'

Will felt startled out of his reverie. 'Just how you never seem to change. Why is that, Olivia?'

'You make it sound like a bad thing.'

They walked side by side to the gallery café and sat down at one of the tables next to the windows overlooking Queen Street.

'Just puzzling.'

'But you like a good puzzle.'

'Actually, someone sent me one the other day.'

'Oh. What of?'

'I don't know. I've only just started it.'

'Emily liked difficult puzzles,' she said quietly. 'Is it difficult?'

'It requires concentration.'

He noticed she was wearing a new ring on her right hand. It was large, garish, not to her taste, a garnet.

'Nice ring.'

Olivia looked at him with her open grey eyes. She held contact for a fraction too long. Her hand touched her neck. He knew people did these things sometimes when they were about to lie.

'A present to myself.'

Who is he? Will wondered. He felt a pang of jealousy, had an instinct that he might be an older man, an academic perhaps. Someone who could talk to her about the symbolism of death in art. Olivia didn't deserve to be alone, not like him. He wasn't sure why this was the case, but he felt it was to do with a way of being. He'd always felt stranded on a rock far out to sea. Olivia was a firm part of society, no matter how alienated she was from herself.

They had used to take Emily around the gallery together, holding her hands, but the young girl would gaze up at the paintings abstractedly. To her, art was petrified life, books were petrified life. Emily was restive in the gallery, wanted to run through the open spaces of the room like an Indian over the prairie.

There was only one painting Emily had liked looking at: an eighteenth-century portrait of a girl in peasant's clothing. The girl had a straightforward, unrefined expression, and an abrupt-looking face as if she had been finished off too quickly. There was nothing lingering or conventionally pretty about her. She was present until she was gone.

The backdrop was a garden wall on which a cat sat looking up at a bird. But the girl looked straight out, and it was difficult to work out if the artist had meant the girl to be like the cat or the bird: victim or predator. Or perhaps, looking into the girl's eyes, she was both. There was always a balance, he thought – humans should remember that balance between victim and predator.

Chapter 6

Will decided to pay another visit to the Ververs' mansion. Lady Verver lived in a set of sprawling rooms at the top of the Gothic house. The rooms were full of chintz and china ornaments but there was a smell of urine combined with talcum powder in the air. Lucy Verver welcomed Will effusively: it seemed she didn't get many visitors. Her white hair was tied up in a bun, strands falling around her pale gaunt cheeks. She looked fragile and she caught the brief look of pity in his eyes.

'Don't feel sorry for me. Age has its recompenses, you know.'

'Such as?'

'I'll leave you to find out that for yourself.'

She smiled to reveal gaps in her teeth, between thin lips. It was as if old age, the persona, was mocking him, laughing at the gap between now and the future, mocking time passing. Time defiantly went forward. Humans were caught in its trajectory like rabbits in headlamps.

'Can you tell me anything about Louise that might explain her disappearance?'

'Of course, it was only a matter of time before she went missing.'

'What do you mean?'

'Hasn't anyone told you? She was very unhappy.'

'I knew she gambled.'

She snorted. 'Of course she did. She gambled with life as well. Took risks. Because she was unhappy. Misery makes people careless with life, with the choices they make. In the last few weeks she didn't know who she was any more. Memories had started to come back. These memories were frightening as well as sad because they weren't joined up. There were no connections. Just images, as if they had been planted in her.'

'She told you this?'

She shook her head. 'She didn't have to. I could see it in her eyes.'

'Do you know what they were? What exactly she was remembering?'

'She'd just say odd things, you know.'

'Like?'

'"Rocking-horse," she said, "I used to have a rocking-horse."'

'Lots of children have rocking-horses.'

'I presumed she was remembering her childhood after having no memory of her childhood at all. Quite extraordinary.'

'And you think that's why she ran away?'

'Well, and Adam of course is difficult.'

'You mean temperamental?'

'He can be very sweet one moment and then say something quite malicious the next. Impossible to live with. He's so clever, you see. He gets bored.'

'Louise bored him?' Will remembered Lord Verver saying his son was infatuated by her.

'Louise never really had a chance. That is the other side

39

to love: the expectation, the demands. The pain whenever your loved ones do not live up to the fantasy imposed upon them. Fallen idols.'

And Will could see that somewhere in Lucy's strained face, she was also talking about herself. Her son had in some way disillusioned her, broken her frail heart.

'You know, my son is a genius. And that comes with great burdens. Emotional fallout.' Here she gave him a hard stare. 'No matter who he is with, his brilliance leaves him fundamentally alone. His ideas are so radical, the scientific establishment won't have anything to do with him. He had to start his computer company, Future Productions, on his own.'

Both of Adam's parents, Will thought, seemed in awe of his brilliance.

'Louise hadn't become involved with anyone else?'

Lucy gave a sly smile. 'You mean another man? She would have been susceptible. I felt sorry for the girl. Adam was so much older. And the type to have been intensely romantic at the beginning until it all wore off, as it were.'

'How did they meet?'

But Lucy suddenly looked down at her feet.

'What I need are some new slippers. These ones are getting so shabby... Would you mind fetching me a drink, dear? My throat has got so dry with all this jabbering.'

William went to a small sink in the corner of the room and took a tooth-glass and filled it with water from the tap. A bar of lavender soap was melting in the plug hole and he prised it out, its soft consistency repulsive. He gave a quick glance round her room. It was full of books, piled up high all around her and on the shelves, books and papers. She saw him looking at them.

'I'm writing my memoirs,' she said. 'I've had such an interesting life. But it's hard work remembering everything that's happened. I have my diaries to help me, of course.' She pointed to a pile of red bound school exercise books, each with a roman numeral on the front.

'I suppose you have to be selective.'

Lucy gave him a stolen look from her childhood, impish like a little girl.

'Oh yes. That's the only way to the truth. To be selective. Otherwise it's all a meaningless jumble, no verity in it at all.'

She sipped the water he had handed her and made an expression of distaste.

'Ugh. It's warm. You should have let the water run.' She gave him another childish smile. 'But you've let me run, haven't you, Mr Blake? Just run on and on. But I'm tired now. It's time for you to go.'

William nodded and saw her eyes flickering, head falling forward in sleep, and left the room, shutting the door quietly on whatever it was she was dreaming.

Chapter 7

The *if only*s were the worst, the small shifts in outcome, any outcome other than the one that had happened. Like opening a book at a certain page, you could easily open it again at a different page. The words would be different but it would be the same book, the same life. Unfortunately, the book had fallen open at the page where the girl went missing, and that was that. However, unlike Will, Olivia accepted the page. Never pleaded for a different page. Read the words that she had been given.

The loss of Emily splintered their marriage like broken shards of glass. They had not fought for their marriage; that which you break you own. No, the opposite: as soon as they had broken it, they disowned it, as if they could not bear to look at their faces reflected in the broken pieces.

The first night they slept in the house after Emily went missing he had dreamt his body was being pulled apart, his limbs falling off one by one until he was only left with phantom pain. Food hardly tasted of anything. Salt, sweet, sour and bitterness, he would taste in his mouth, but no other flavours.

As time passed, he had to fight off the lowering feeling in his head, in his face, in his limbs, as if he were walking through mud. The feeling started off imperceptibly and then grew stronger and stronger as if the opposite of bleeding to death, as if he was filling more and more with thick, viscous blood until it was engulfing his lungs and he was drowning.

Olivia retreated from the marriage into her work, for what was loss of marital love anyway compared to the loss of a child. Outwardly she was not affected by grief. But she lost all desire. The sensation of his lips seemed to repulse her. It was as if her skin had transformed from an organ that could receive pleasure to one that repulsed it – that was what it had felt like, as if the whole surface of her body had turned to sandpaper.

Seeing other children only caused Will further pain. In the days after Emily's disappearance Will could only think, how dare other children who were not her, how dare they be here in this time and space *at this moment* when Emily is not. It was as if these children were dancing on her grave. A grave that she didn't even have. There was no specific place to mourn. No place where they could go and place flowers.

Will did not believe in God or an afterlife. But he believed in the importance of ritual and myth. The need and impulse of man to tell a story, make a pattern. He knew of the importance of laying to rest, of bringing something to an end – but how could they, without the certainty of a grave? It meant grief was located all around them, in the air they breathed, the water they bathed in, the food they ate. There was no one place where they knew Emily to be. So she was everywhere.

He had once loved jazz, its sinuous improvisation, snaking away, making connections and leaps like the process of thought itself. But it now sounded brash, crass, inconsequential like a series of notes on piano or trumpet played by the tone-deaf. However, he could hear the drums: the drums seemed to leap out at him, their repetitive quality not a pattern, but a sound, like the beating of his remorseless heart.

And then – he never thought it would happen – life became less hard to live. A year after the loss of Emily, six months after Olivia finally left him, the moment came when Will fell in love with his own solitude. He would take himself for a meal. Watch television with himself. Have a drink with himself. Point out to himself the exquisite flatness of the sea. It wasn't a solipsistic world: he didn't think much about himself at all. There was just that residual self-pity that followed him around like a lame dog, to remind him he was human.

There was something about depression, he thought, that if you were lucky enough to come out the other end, made you a kind of visionary – like drugs, it was mind-altering. It seemed to give another dimension to reality, a fuller version of it, as if previously the world had seemed a theatrical stage-show of colour. It forged you.

Desire returned with a vengeance, a ferocity. An abstract desire connected to pornography, rather than feeling. Most people lived life in disguise, concealing their own wants so as not to seem greedy. But we were all greedy in the end, greedy for different things. It was part of our humanity.

He was powerless over his desire. He would drive down to Leith harbour where he would see the prostitutes walking up and down the streets, some looking as young as twelve in the semi-darkness, their faces always turning towards the light of a car like moths towards a flame. They would always make eye contact, a strange eye contact – dead certain. As if to say, I am a certainty: if you want certainty here I am, dressed in tight clothes, my breasts swelling visibly underneath, the thighs exposed, certainty in every ounce of visible flesh, reality at its most naked.

The prostitutes he had against walls in deserted alleyways that smelt of previous sex, the ecstasy of the momentary – he would do anything for that moment, make whatever sacrifice necessary to satisfy himself. The compulsion of desire over reason never ceased to amaze him. The sex was an urgent powerful release. It was authentic.

He would be careful never to choose the same prostitute. Nor did he ask for conversation. He had heard too many stories of the low life to want to hear any more from the mouths of prostitutes. He was storied out. The abuse, the drink, the drugs. If there were only seven plots in the whole world, poverty had all of them. Their young skin concealed their history, their past, like onion skins made of the sheets of old tabloids. He was always tender and they could not help but be hard back: heroin ran through their veins like ice. The only conversation involved the transaction of money.

~

A swan had walked right up to the beach and was standing by the wall of the promenade; it looked like it was waiting for something. It looked sinister, unnatural, a lone swan far up the beach at low tide, its beady eyes watching. Had it become separated from the others, Will wondered, had it got lost? Had it been abandoned? What had happened to Louise?

The block of huge luxury flats were white and conspicuous on the promenade, seeming as if they had landed down from outer space, alien. Large balconies overlooked the beach. He rang the intercom to Adam's flat.

'It's Will Blake.'

'Come on up.'

Will climbed the white marble steps, different from the usual dark stone steps of the tenement blocks of Portobello. Adam had the penthouse flat at the top, the biggest and the grandest. When Will entered, Adam moved toward him to shake his hand as if his body were an appendage, slightly behind the speed of his thoughts.

The flat was white and minimalist with black leather chrome seats scattered over golden wooden floors. Will was immediately struck by how male it was: adult male. There were no signs of women or children and the only touch of femininity was a large crystal glass vase filled with erect white irises. There was no sign of disorder here, everything was in its place – everything except Louise. The rugs lay in perfect symmetry, perfectly lined to the edges of the walls. It was a place of rectangles – there were no books, no decorations, only an unfinished game of chess on a desk and a rather incongruous paperweight on a side-table.

Will picked it up. Snow fell down on a little scene. It showed an old-fashioned detective, a trilby on his head, encased in a heavy overcoat walking through a snowscaped city.

There was a circularity and self-referential aspect to the case that troubled him. His ability to solve cases depended on being unseen, a watcher unobserved. Were these references to himself – as in Louise's address book, or the paperweight – just coincidences? Perhaps he was trying to create patterns out of chance, find significance in the random. He had to sift out deliberate intention from happenstance. Perhaps he had become oversensitive to a design that didn't really exist. Coincidences, as always, were traps for the unmindful and the superstitious.

Will looked down through the window. He saw the blind man walking down the promenade and shouted down to him. The blind man, recognizing Will's voice, looked up in his direction and waved. He could easily have heard the argument between husband and wife from down there, Will thought.

'I don't think you'll find anything here to help you,' Adam was saying. 'Louise didn't need things. Things just attach you to the past.'

'And she didn't have a past…What happened, exactly?'

'You mean, how did she lose her memory? It was before we met. A car accident.'

'How did you meet?'

'In hospital. Part of my research into artificial intelligence involves computers and memories. I was interested in meeting someone who had lost hers.' His voice was languid, drawled, but his words were very precise, reflecting the exactness of his thoughts.

Will had met people like him before, people whose synapses fired more quickly, got the joke a second before other people. They were like another species, living amongst mere mortals. But Adam needed him, needed him to act out his plans, be the physical presence of his ideas, to find out where his wife had gone.

'You've always been interested in AI?' Will asked.

'Computers don't have motives, they don't want anything from you. Humans have their own desires and needs, that's what makes them so difficult. With machines you don't have to try and work out what they want. They just give and give. Like whores.'

Adam smiled at Will and for a mad moment Will thought,

he knows intuitively I pay for sex. He can see it in my eyes.

Will shook the paperweight and watched the snow settle on the lonely figure. He turned it upside down. The name *William Blake* was engraved in tiny writing underneath. The paperweight slipped through his fingers and broke on the shiny wooden floor, shards of glass and liquid scattering across it.

Chapter 8

As Adam gazed bemusedly at him, Will tried to apologize. 'I'm sorry,' he said. 'It slipped from my fingers.'

'Don't worry, it's just a piece of tat Louise bought.'

Will had thought it looked out of place in the flat. 'Did she engrave the name?'

'What name?'

'My name is on the bottom.'

Adam smiled, vaguely contemptuous.

'You must be seeing things, Mr Blake. Why on earth would your name be on the bottom of our paperweight?'

Will bent down and slowly picked up the pieces, carefully checking each shard of glass, but he could find no lettering at all. He must have hallucinated the words. He picked up the little detective that was unharmed and lying under the sofa.

'But this *is* the figure of a detective.'

'I suppose it is. Like you are.' This time his smile was supercilious.

'When did she buy it?'

'Well, now you mention it, she bought it quite recently. About a week before she went missing. She brought it back from the centre of town. She said it had just caught her eye.'

'But you said she wasn't interested in things.'

'That's what I said.' His reply was too quick.

'So it must have meant something special to her.'

'I suppose so.' He smiled. Like Olivia, Adam was a player of chess. He liked intellectual games. There was something about this he seemed to be enjoying.

'Is there anyone she might have gone to who she trusted?'

'There's always Miles.'

'Who's Miles?'

'He's Mrs Elliot's son. Miles would do anything for Louise. She treats him like a son. If she gets in touch with anyone, it will be Miles. It makes me think she can't have gone far. But you'll be lucky to get anything out of him. I've already tried.'

Adam strode over to the other side of the room and opened a door. A boy sat in the corner of a study playing on a computer. It was the same boy Will had seen outside the arcade with Mikael, and later, giving the package to the singer.

'He spends most of his time over here. Playing the latest Future Productions game, *Oracle*.'

Miles didn't register Will. He was more interested in the reality on the screen. Looking at the game, Miles's eyes had a vacant look, as if all thought had been taken out and a series of beguiling flashes had replaced them. It occurred to Will that the boy was not playing the computer; the computer was, expertly and insidiously, playing him. Miles had become a reactive machine responding to each twitch on the screen. The boy had become a vehicle for the computer's imagination.

Machines were busy making us in their own image, Will thought. There was no conspiracy involved. We had done it to ourselves. We were simplifying our lives, making ourselves more receptive to the straightforward mechanisms of reward and desire. Complexity had become inefficient. And here was the result: an adolescent boy as far removed from consciousness as any piece of redundant machinery in a junkyard.

Will bent over the boy and accidentally knocked over a vase of irises next to the computer. The water spilled out in a pool over the burnished mahogany desk. Still the boy didn't notice him, so Will leant over and switched off his game. The first response of the boy was an angry glare, pure fury at his drug being removed. Will had read that computer game manufacturers employed addiction counsellors to make their games more compulsive.

'I need to ask you some questions about Louise.'

The boy seemed so zoned out, he half-expected him to ask, *Who?*

'She's been missing a week now. Have you any idea where she might have gone?'

The boy shrugged his shoulders. 'Can I switch on my game, now?'

'Sure ... in a minute... How do you play *Oracle*?'

'You ask it questions.'

'Have you asked where Louise is?'

'No.'

'Why not?'

'She's okay.'

'But what if something has happened to her?'

'It hasn't,' Miles replied.

'How do you know?'

'I just do.'

Does he, Will thought, does he know for certain, does he perhaps even know where she is? It explained his lack of concern about her. The boy stared at him, a slight dull resistance, as if shutting out any further queries, any expectation of elaboration. Will knew further questions

51

would be pointless. He had an instinct for knowing what was and was not possible. Miles switched on his game again.

Will no longer felt sure what was happening, as if in some subtle way the world had become an hallucinatory vision. The people he was meeting weren't in full control of their impulses. Adam was compelled by his search for his wife, the boy by his games, Louise by her gambling in the arcade. They all seemed inclined towards danger. Danger was attracted to weakness, not strength; danger came and filled in the gaps, like water following the easiest routes down to the sea.

When Will returned to the living room, Adam was on the phone, standing with his back to him. Glancing down at Adam's desk, Will saw the same brown envelope he had seen earlier on the hall table at Lord and Lady Ververs' house. He noticed the envelope was postmarked a few days after Louise had gone missing. Without stopping to think what he was doing, he picked the envelope up and slipped it quickly underneath his coat, shutting the door quietly behind him as he left.

Down below on the promenade, Will pulled out the grainy colour photographs. They were all of Adam walking down a street. Just ahead of him was walking a petite and voluptuous woman; it wasn't Louise. It was a woman with long raven-black hair, dark eyes and full red lips. She had a strong face with an old vulnerability, as if life had ravaged her but a certain perceptiveness had seen her through. She looked, he thought, old-fashioned.

The photos had been taken at various different times and she was in all of them. Adam, for whatever reason, had always wanted her. In the background of one or two photos was a shadowy Victorian building. She walked in the way a prostitute walks with a client, the prostitute slightly ahead as if the client didn't exist, but the velocity of both their movements intent on the same mission: sex. It was as if they didn't want to know each other but they were walking separately to the same end.

So Adam visited prostitutes too, Will thought. Perhaps there were more similarities between himself and Adam than seemed apparent. Will turned the photographs over. On the back of one of them was written in an illiterate hand, *What have you done with her?*

Who had sent the photographs? Who did the "her" refer to? Not to Louise – Adam would not have employed him to find her if he had had anything to do with her disappearance. No, combined with the note, the photos seemed to constitute blackmail – tell the blackmailer where this "her" is, or some of these photos will be sent to your wife.

~

Will was sitting in the Chinese family's café, lost in thought, when he became vaguely aware of a woman taking her seat at the table next to him. He didn't want to look at her directly and when he finally did look round, as if to look out of the window, he caught a glimpse of her face. It had the almost-oriental-shaped perfection of Louise Verver's. She was engrossed in reading a book. The title read *Songs of Innocence and of Experience*. Before he could stop her, Louise had stood up abruptly and left the café. Will hurriedly paid his bill and rushed out after her. He looked up and down the promenade, but she had apparently disappeared into thin air.

Frantically he ran along the side streets, searching for her in vain. He returned dejected to the café where her abandoned book still lay on the table. It was wide open at the page she had been reading:

THE SICK ROSE

O, rose, thou art sick;
The invisible worm
That flies in the night,
In the howling storm,

Has found out thy bed
Of crimson joy,
And his dark secret love
Does thy life destroy.

But as he read, the words kept disappearing until he was left with a blank page. He flicked through the rest of the book; all the pages were now blank. Only the title and author's name on the front remained. He staggered out of the café, leaving the book on the table, and collapsed onto the pavement outside.

He came to on the kerb, a kindly old woman looking anxiously into his eyes.

'Take a fall, did you, love?'

Will couldn't speak. He nodded. Yes, he thought, I have taken a fall – I no longer wait for them to be given to me.

Olivia had told him not to blame himself for Emily going missing. He had been with her when she had disappeared. He had left her just for a moment on the small wall that bordered the promenade, the wall between the concrete and the sand.

Chapter 9

The blind man was walking down the promenade on a dry day; no sun and no rain, a kind of blank day where the world was waiting in purgatory. His dog by his side, his white cane moved from side to side in expert flicks. The blind man looked so alert that Will was again struck by the odd sensation that he could actually see. He seemed to have a golden light around him as if he were actually glowing, light pouring from the pores of his skin in a radiant ambience. Will felt heat emanating from him through the cool air onto his face like the sun.

He came to a stop as he approached Will.

'Any luck?' he asked.

'How do you know it's me?' Will replied.

'Your distinctive smell. Whisky and salt.'

'I'm going to have to wash more often.'

The young man beckoned towards him. Will bent his head forward and the blind man whispered in his ear. 'I've just remembered. I smelt him. I'm sure I did. Adam always smells of irises. For the past few months, once every week, always coming out of the same place.'

'Where?'

'The Milton Hotel.'

Will knew what the Milton Hotel was a cover for and having seen the photos of Adam with the prostitute, some of the jigsaw pieces fell into place.

'Are you sure?'

'Unmistakable. He was coming out of the garden.'

'There could have been irises growing.'

'At this time of year? Besides, there are no flowers in the Milton's garden.'

He was right. The hotel was a huge Victorian house on the promenade, its garden a rough patch of lawn with a slide and swing for customers' children. Customers could drink at the tables and benches on the lawn which was raised so they could look over the promenade to the beach and sea. The occasional sailboat or oil tanker would lie on the horizon.

~

The Milton had a pub downstairs and signs at the entrance telling people what not to do. It also had a large staircase leading up to the bedrooms on the first floor where the prostitutes worked. There was the smell of dust and dankness in the Milton Hotel. Not so much the smell of sex but of vacated souls. Souls that had just got up and left. Will did not find the smell repulsive, rather evocative of a different kind of life from that of everyday living. Society had locked hard sexuality away in dank rooms because it couldn't face it in the light of day. The Milton Hotel was the dark red mirror of love.

The man behind the bar downstairs was louche and attentive, tall, with lugubrious eyes in a long thin face.

'And what can I do for you, Mr Blake? It's a long time since we've had the pleasure of your company.'

The rows of bottles along the bar twinkled as the sunlight

poured over them making the golden and copper liquids inside glisten.

'I'm looking for a missing person.'

Sean put a glass on the bar and poured Will a small dram. Will looked at the liquid in the glass. Yes, definitely the colour of copper.

'And who might the missing person be?' Sean asked in his Irish lilt.

'A young woman. Louise Verver.'

With his high cheekbones, Sean must have been very handsome once, like a race horse, with those dark brown eyes and floppy dark hair the only remnants of his youth. But now his dark skin was pockmarked and there were deep lines etched round his eyes where he had smiled too much.

'Never heard of her.'

'She's about five-four. Brunette, brown eyes, symmetrical features.'

Sean smiled. 'Like the tiger.'

Will took a swig of his whisky.

'So how come I haven't seen you around?'

'I decided to give it a rest. Needed time on my own.'

'We've missed you.'

'You always had a way with words, Sean.'

'So has she done anything she shouldn't have?'

'Not as far as I know. Strange family, though!'

'Aren't they all.'

'I think she may be mixed up in something. Difficult to say. She's the wife of Adam Verver.'

'Ah, the mad scientist. In the new white flats?'

Will nodded. 'He's come here?'

'Tricky character.'

'Can you expand on that?'

'Not really.' The Irishman gave him another smile. 'But I wouldn't trust him, if I were you.'

'Or if I were you?'

'That's right.'

You had to be patient with Sean. He went at his own speed of disclosure. He didn't take kindly to being hurried. If you hurried him it was as if you were stepping on his time with muddy footprints. Some people got bored quickly, wanted information at speed. Sean would take it as an obscure insult, a mark of disrespect. To try and abbreviate that time was both hurtful to his world view and a personal injury.

Will showed him the picture of Adam and the prostitute. 'Know her?'

'Never seen her.' Sean hadn't looked at the picture.

'She doesn't work for you, then?'

Sean still didn't look at it.

'Nope.'

'That building in the background looks like the Milton.'

He finally looked at it; his expression didn't change.

'So it does.' He looked up, still the same indifferent look in his eyes. 'Is this leading anywhere?'

'Hopefully upstairs so I can meet some of the girls.'

Sean wiped the counter. He rinsed some glasses and dried them.

'Just go up. You know where to find them. In the room marked *Waiting Room*.'

Will climbed up the wide carpeted stairs. Outside the window that faced out to the promenade, he could see the grey plateau of sea. A flock of seagulls cawed loudly in the sky. He wondered if the little Chinese girl was feeding them again.

He passed an aspidistra on the landing and reached the first floor which had rows of doors on either side. On one side the doors were named with various girls' names: Coral, Trixie, Lolita and Rose. On the other side the doors just had numbers. He knocked on the middle door with the sign *Waiting Room* on it.

Inside a woman was reclining on a burgundy velvet sofa. Her face had the flat round features of the young: about sixteen or seventeen, he thought. She had auburn hair and green eyes and was wearing cheap transparent lingerie. He could see through the pale blue nylon her full white breasts and erect pearl-like nipples. Will had to concentrate on what he was doing there.

She stood up and leant provocatively against the wall.

'I'm Rose. Interested?'

'I am interested. But not in the way you think. I'm looking for her.' He showed her the photo of Adam and the prostitute. She smiled. A smile that opened up her face, and her prettiness made him indescribably sad. She had endearingly crooked teeth.

'You want Belle? She's not here today. Won't I do instead?' She looked at him coquettishly.

'Not at the moment. I need to ask her some questions.'

'You can ask me any question you want.'

She smiled at him suggestively. Will took a breath.

'It's about a missing woman. Louise. Her husband Adam Verver has been known to visit Belle. I need to ask Belle some questions about him.'

'You won't get anything from her.'

'I can try.'

'No, you don't get it. She's a junkie.'

59

'But she'll be able to make herself understood?'

'Oh, she'll be able to make herself understood.'

Will was growing tired of the constant sexual innuendo. The girl was young. She was just doing her job. It was depressing.

'This is serious.'

'It always is.'

'Can you tell me where Belle lives, then?' This seemed to be a trajectory towards madness.

She shrugged her naked shoulders. 'Milton Hotel, Room 14 is the only address for her that I know. She's had a room here since she's worked.'

'She lives here alone?'

'She does now. She used to share with her daughter, Jade. Before she went missing.'

'When was this?'

'A few months ago. The girl never came back from school. She was only seven.'

All the missing, Will thought. People went missing in the underworld of Portobello and no one batted an eyelid. Just an old photo on a lamppost. Who cares about the missing daughter of a prostitute?

'Do you know where Belle is at the moment? I need to talk to her.'

She shrugged her shoulders again. It was becoming a habit.

'You'd better go,' she said. 'I'm expecting a client soon.'

Will went down to the landing and stood behind the aspidistra. He watched as Rose returned to her own room, then quickly climbed the stairs again and, using a credit card, entered No. 14. At first glance the room looked innocuous, like a pink frilly room in a Bed and Breakfast, but on closer inspection there were the odd details that meant it could only be a room for sex. A pair of handcuffs left under a chair, an unused condom lying under the bed, boxes of tissues... A small photo of Belle's daughter Jade, with her eager-to-please smile, sat on the bedside table.

He opened the drawer to the bedside table. There were a few recent receipts and a matchbox. The receipts were all for meals at a café-restaurant called Americana at the top of Leith Walk. The meals were all taken at the same time – seven-ish. Will looked at his watch. It was about six-thirty.

Chapter 10

Will drove up Leith Walk and parked behind the diner. *Americana* was written in large neon lettering above the doors and through the grey rain of Edinburgh the highly lit interior looked enticing. As he entered he saw that a self-service buffet lay to the right of a series of cubicled upholstered seats. The rainy dreary street with the cars rushing by could be seen clearly through the large glass walls. The place was empty except for a very large man in a chef's once-white, brown-stained uniform standing behind the cashier's desk. He looked proud and his pale skin greasy.

Will ordered a black coffee and sat down on a seat over-looking the pavement outside. These places had a narcotic effect. But Will liked to daydream. He had almost finished his coffee when the glass door opened and an elegantly dressed woman in high heels entered. Her pitch-black hair was tied loosely back. She was looking for someone. He could see in her eyes a dark intuition as she looked slowly round the room. Her eyes rested on him for a moment and then glanced away. She looked more sensual in real life.

He tried to remain oblivious. He took a sip from his now-lukewarm coffee as he watched Belle order a glass of beer and sit down in the cubicle in front of him. He was looking at her graceful back. She had avoided eye contact as she passed him.

He would never have guessed she was a prostitute. Except

for the fact she was alone – prostitutes often seemed alone, even when they were with their customers. They had an apartness about them, either existential or desperate. Or drug-induced.

She was wearing a tailored cream dress which clung to her hourglass figure. She looked like she was waiting for someone; she kept checking her watch impatiently. Having finished her drink, she sighed, picked up her bag, and put on her coat. Will quickly stood up and paid the bill. He caught sight of himself in the reflection of the window – he looked hungry for sex, a stalker.

He followed Belle out into the night. The lights all around were reflected in the black puddles. It was still raining and Will put up his umbrella. Belle was walking up Leith Walk towards Queen Street. She had put on a transparent macintosh so that he could see the shape of her figure through the plastic sheen. The plastic also reflected the streetlights in a way that made her body a flickering screen of luminosity.

She walked in a hurry, as if being pulled along by her idea of the immediate future. She walked along Queen Street to the National Portrait Gallery. To his surprise she stopped at the door. It was now 8.15 on a Friday night. The gallery shut at five. However, wardens were on duty throughout the night; perhaps she had come to see one of them. She rang the small brass bell on the left and Will watched as the gallery's wooden door opened and Belle slipped through.

He rang the bell and blagged his way in, saying he had to collect something for Olivia. The warden on the door, a grey-haired man in a blue uniform with a quizzical smile, nodded. He had known Will since he had first dated Olivia. The warden was a template of time passing.

'You know where her office is, Mr Blake.'

Will walked into the elegant entrance hall, full of pillars and sculptures. It was not a place where you would usually find any women portrayed in works of art, let alone a prostitute. The portrait gallery was a haven of the Edinburgh upper and middle classes. It housed the portraits of the elite: scientists and writers. What was her connection to the gallery?

He could hear the rain tapping down on the roof. Olivia's office was on the third floor and he swiftly climbed the soft, low carpeted steps, passing on each landing the large rooms with the portraits of the dead all around. On each landing he hoped for a glimpse of Belle.

He knew that, as CCTV cameras were carefully positioned about the gallery, he had to look as if he were doing what he'd said he would. He walked through the antiquaries library, a neo-Gothic wood-panelled room with glass bookcases, to reach Olivia's office on the other side.

Her office was as tidy as ever, every article and magazine meticulously laid out. The walls were lined with heavy hard-backed books of art, not the light detective paperbacks he preferred to read. A large photo of Emily stood on the desk, smiling out, a school photo, its clarity and brashness only adding to the brightness of her soul. Whenever he saw a picture of Emily such a wave of anguish washed over him he felt as if he were drowning.

Olivia, however, had never seemed to miss Emily. He was overwhelmed by the sudden feeling that he didn't really know her. He absentmindedly picked up a paper on her desk entitled *Innocence and Experience in Eighteenth-Century Paintings of Children*. His ex-wife's article was written in immaculate type with perfect margins, every comma in place. Olivia had always possessed an exquisite attention to detail. He read the first paragraph: "Children depicted in the art of the eighteenth century can be presented in innocent poses that sometimes disguise the erotic nature of both impoverished and privileged childhoods."

What devastating ideas written in such academic prose. What a travesty learning could make of reality; it was an illusion, a conjuring trick. He briefly thought of Emily and what terror she must have felt. Then his mind went blank, a white void that wiped reality clean.

He was about to leave the room when he noticed *Where were you?! Belle xx* scrawled on the last page of Olivia's article. It was in the same illiterate hand as the blackmail note on the back of the photograph of Adam and Belle and on the 'missing person' poster of Jade. He ran his finger over the biro ink – it smudged, it was still wet. Had it been *Olivia* Belle had been waiting for in Americana?

The CCTV camera was filming him. He pretended to look for the thing that wasn't there before leaving the room, shutting the door behind him. It was then that he saw Belle disappearing round the corner of the stairs like Alice down the rabbit-hole but by the time he got to the bottom of the stairs, she had gone.

The fresh air outside invigorated him after the muggy interior of the Portrait Gallery. Its mustiness and sense of dead history oppressed him. It was all about the past, mummified. But Belle had been a disturbing aura in there, a breath of life, a latent energy that had disrupted the suffocating atmosphere of the place.

The next morning he was woken up by the phone ringing – it was Olivia.

'What were you doing in my office, Will?'

That tight clipped voice. He looked at the time. It was 9am. He imagined her at her desk, precisely clothed, back upright, face set. He decided not to ask her about Belle; he didn't want to involve Olivia in his work unnecessarily.

'I'm sorry, Olivia. I had to get into the gallery.'

'Well, next time have the grace to phone me first, before you use my name as some trumped-up excuse to get in the building.'

'My name wouldn't have worked so well.'

'What were you doing?'

He could hear her clock the hesitation in his voice.

'Work. I can't talk about it.'

'Actually, I'd rather not know.' That familiar irritation in her voice.

'It's just too complicated.'

'It's always too complicated, Will. Why can't things ever be simple?'

He laughed, with a brief wave of affection for her. It would always be there.

'I've got to go, Olivia. I won't use your name again.'

'Bye, William.'

He hung up. He was still in bed. He lay looking up at the ceiling. It needed painting – white paint was peeling off the surface. A damp patch like a map of Africa was growing in the corner. At least the rain wasn't actually dripping through.

Chapter 11

The phone rang and Will picked it up to hear Adam sobbing down the phone.

'What's happened?'

'I can hardly say it – she's dead ... dead.'

'Louise? They've found her?'

'NO. No. My mother. Father discovered her.'

He sounded distraught and Will get could no more sense from him.

It was Miles' mother, Mrs Elliot, who let Will in, and he followed her upstairs to Lucy Verver's quarters where she was lying curled up in the foetal position on the floor. Her pale scalp, fragile as eggshell, was visible through her thinning hair, the grey hairs lying like threads over her skin, matted with blood where a heavy instrument had hit her. Her shirt had wrenched up and William could see that her bare ribs were bruised and mottled. Her room had been turned upside-down, the china dogs lying in pieces on the ground with newspapers scattered all around.

Will noticed that her pile of diaries had been disturbed. He flicked through them: her rural childhood, her debutante balls. Then he looked for this year's diary. It had gone. Will checked around the room, behind the upturned tables, between the bookcases – but nothing. There was no sign of the diary. Someone had deliberately taken it and they had known what year they'd needed.

Lord Verver was sitting in his wheelchair in the conservatory tending a plant when Will approached him.

'I'm very sorry, Lord Verver.'

Verver didn't reply, he just kept on stroking the leaves of a plant between his dry long fingers.

'We must get the roof of the conservatory fixed. It leaks. Where it meets the wall of the house. See?'

He pointed upwards and Will could indeed see a gap.

'When did you last see her?'

'Last night. We had supper together in the dining room, as we always do. Lamb chops and peas, then pudding. She ate well. Nothing seemed wrong.'

'Perhaps we just don't get it yet.'

'Let me know when you do "get" it then, won't you?'

His patrician face became consumed by fury and his pale eyes protruded – rage-watery eyes.

The detective wondered what Verver would do if enraged to a point beyond his control. Anger was what often led to death. People became possessed. He was a physically weak man but his arms were muscular. They looked bizarrely strong in relation to the rest of his puny body.

William was genuinely shocked by Lucy Verver's death. Death always shocked him, as if it was an unnatural alien event. Yet death came to us all, Will thought; murder just made it come that little bit quicker.

'And you heard no one enter the house at night?'

'I fell asleep at eleven. I sleep fitfully. I'm sure I would have heard someone enter.'

'There were no signs of forced entry?'

He shook his head. For the first time his eyes seemed

fearful.

'So how do you think they got in?' Will asked.

'I don't know. Isn't that your job?'

Will didn't reply.

'How many keys do you have?'

'Just three – mine, my wife's, and the housekeeper's.'

'Your son doesn't have one?'

'Why should he? Mary is always in.'

Will felt he was lying.

'How long have you known your housekeeper?'

'She has been in the service of our family for years. She was Adam's nanny, too.'

Coming downstairs, he noticed a portrait hanging above the stairs of Lucy Verver in her younger days. She was wearing a blue jumper with pearls and a mid-length tweed skirt. She had on a silver bracelet and watch and everything was painted in pastel blue, yellow and pink. She sat on the sofa, her flaxen hair falling down around her shoulders. She had been beautiful.

He bumped into Mrs Elliot in the hall.

'It's just terrible,' she said.

This time, he thought, she looked genuinely distressed.

'Lord Verver says you've been in his service for a long time. That you used to look after Adam.'

Defensiveness immediately filled her eyes.

'He was a very good boy, always a good boy,' she said hurriedly.

Mrs Elliot was a very silly woman, Will thought, and he disliked silliness. It seemed to Will a very dangerous characteristic to have. It could do damage. And he wondered if under Mrs Elliot's silliness lay something more sinister.

'I wasn't suggesting otherwise, Mrs Elliot.'

'Oh, but I think you were, Mr Blake.'

And under her fluttering exterior, a look of such extraordinary shrewdness leapt out of her eyes, it almost took his breath away. Every member of this household seemed to be hiding something, he thought.

Will came out into the garden and saw Miles, his fair hair shining in the sun, looking up at a conker tree.

'Hello there,' Will said.

The boy turned around. Will was taken aback by the look of grumpiness on his face. Away from the computer it seemed to be his natural expression and he felt sorry for the boy. He didn't know how to be happy in the outside world.

'Great conker you have there.'

Miles looked down at his hand as if noticing the conker lying there for the first time.

Will took it from him; the unbearably smooth chestnut brown, perfect of its kind, so soft and hard at the same time. Better than any work of art, he thought, a ripe conker.

'Did you notice anything odd last night?'

'Something did wake me up about two. A scream. Then I heard the front door shut. I looked out of the window.'

'Did you see anything?'

'I saw a man walking down the promenade – actually, he was running.'

'Did you recognize him?'

'It was too dark. Some of the lamplight bulbs on the prom need replacing – do you think Lucy being murdered is connected with Louise going missing?'

'Could be.'

'If Louise has gone missing, it's because she wants to,'

Miles added. He seemed completely unconcerned by Lady Verver's death.

'Why do you say that?'

'Because she told me. Just before she left.'

'What exactly did she say?' Will tried to keep the excitement out of his voice. In his experience with people, especially children, it was best to be as neutral as possible when questioning them. Any emotion seemed to put them off. People's natural inclination was to resist intensity.

Miles frowned, as if trying to remember the exact words. When thinking, he looked more gentle, as if thoughts expressed the core of him, made him forget to be moody.

'She said, "It will soon be time for me to go."'

'And you took that to mean she was going to run away?'

'I suppose so.' The boy looked doubtful. 'What else could it have meant?'

'Quite. Quite,' Will said quickly, not wanting to continue his line of thought for fear of upsetting him. Her words could have meant that she had been planning her disappearance, that she had gone of her own volition. They could also mean that she had been planning her death.

~

'Well, it's Will,' Olivia said, standing opposite him in the Portrait Gallery looking like a Byzantine work of art, two-dimensional and iconic. She also sounded ironic. He wondered how she could keep her irony up, like a kite flying in a sky just before dusk after the wind had dropped.

Emily, he thought, had been far more like him than Olivia. She had been passionate, she had understood, she had been

71

a little echo of him. And now, after she had gone, he had become an echo of her.

'What are you doing here?' Olivia continued, mock-astonished.

'It's the anniversary.'

She paused for a moment and then her face went blank. He brushed a loose hair from her forehead. She put up her hand and grabbed his and kept it for a moment by her forehead. He felt a leap of the heart, of hope, but as if sensing this, she at once dropped his hand.

'Of course,' she said. 'Another year since she's gone.'

A child ran across the hallway laughing.

Olivia took his hand. 'I'm sorry, William... Is that the only reason you came?'

He looked at her cold fragility, that mixture of invulnerability and a suggestion that one day she could crack into pieces.

'What other reason could there be?'

Olivia smiled faintly.

Later in the restaurant, eating lunch, she took some bread from the basket. All her movements were so graceful because she was so studied. She saw him looking at her and he immediately lowered his eyes. Olivia put her hand on his.

'How are you, Will? You look strained.'

He tried to rearrange his face, look more upbeat.

'It's just this case. It seems complicated. I feel involved.'

'But that's against the rules.' She smiled.

'I know. It's just got under my skin. The family involved. A strange family.'

He held her hand.

'And you're not strange?' she asked

'Oh, I'm ordinary. Detectives have to be.'

'We will find Emily,' Olivia said. He noted a tone in her voice he had never heard before, more deeply resonant as if was coming from her lungs rather than throat.

'Olivia, that is what you choose to believe.'

Anger lit up her eyes.

'Don't you understand what I'm saying, Will? We will find her alive.' And then quickly she got up. 'I've got to get back to my work.'

'Are you sure it misses you that much?'

She smiled. 'More than you do.'

'Don't be so sure.'

He gave her a clumsy hug and there was Olivia walking out of the restaurant in front of him, the other murmurs of the diners unaffected, all desire between them spent a long time ago. He waited a minute and then stumbled out of the restaurant into the chilly afternoon.

Edinburgh had that cold windy air that was impossible to argue with. It took him by the scruff of the neck and buffeted him down Queen Street. Sometimes he felt that Edinburgh, the centre of Scotland's power, held like an oracle all his secrets in its heart. That if he just walked round the grand self-important squares of the New Town for long enough on a cold afternoon with a sunless sky, all the answers would be given him.

Chapter 12

Will decided to go for a walk on the promenade. As the sound of the seagulls with their melancholy laughter echoed in his ears, he saw Louise Verver again walking along one of the wooden groins that intersected the beach at regular intervals to stop the sand washing away. Like wooden walls, they reached out taller and taller into the sea but at low tide looked like broken shipwrecks. Her very neutrality had a powerful effect on him, as if he were suddenly standing in a desert watching her walk away. He wanted to run over and touch her, to make sure she wasn't actually a mirage.

Just at that moment he was distracted by a dog starting to bark at his feet and he turned round to see the blind man. He quickly looked back to the groin she had been walking along but she had gone. He scoured the beach dotted with sparse walkers but could see her nowhere. He turned back to the man.

'Have you found her yet?' the blind man asked.

'No.' William couldn't admit to these visions. He didn't want to admit his constant failure to catch them in his hands and make them real.

'You sound shaken.'

Will thought he had sounded in control.

The man gave the dog a pat on his head. 'Why don't you ask the oracle?'

The oracle stood at the end of the promenade near the sewage works. It was a machine in the shape of a high priestess, with snakes for hair and a Greek tunic. A kind of automated fortune-teller. She was standing on a neon-lit box with a light bulb in the centre of it and a slot near the bottom of the box for the questions and replies. Above the slot was written in mock ancient Greek lettering, *Know Thyself*.

That night, Will walked along the promenade. It was deadly still and the lamplights led him down towards the oracle. The sea was quiet and the moon low in the black sky. The flashing lighthouse on the island swept over the water in a long white beam. The dry, cold air caught his throat and stung his face. He could hear the tune, *Mister Sandman* going round and round in his head.

Will came to the oracle and put a pound coin in the oracle's outstretched hand. He heard a whirring sound and out of the box popped a thin blank card. He wrote on it, *Why do I have these visions of Louise Verver?* and slipped it back in the slot in the box.

Three minutes later he received the oracle's answer. The writing was clearly typed out, in the old-fashioned typeface of a 1930s film-noir typewriter, as if the answer had been written a long time before he had asked the question. *Because she doesn't know why she wants you to find her.* He folded the card carefully, running his nail down the paper to make a clean line, and put it in his pocket.

~

'Can I have an ice-cream?' Emily had asked. She had previously hurt her foot on some glass buried in the sand, so she knew she had bartering power. He didn't buy her ice-creams often, especially not on cold days.

'Stay there and rest your foot,' he had said. The kiosk was only a hundred yards up the promenade.

If it hadn't been for that hidden shard of glass she would have skipped along beside him, asking if she could have a chocolate flake as well. Instead she had sat nursing her foot, staring at him soulfully as he walked away.

He often wondered about that piece of glass and how it had got there. A little piece of burnished sand that had caused such irrevocable grief. The thought of it now pierced his heart like Kay's in *The Snow Queen*. He had looked back once or twice on the way to the kiosk to see her still sitting on the wall. He remembered thinking how self-contained she looked but if there had been any justice in the world he would have turned and walked back, carried her on his shoulders or woven her a flying carpet so she could have accompanied him those yards. But instead he walked on, her vulnerability a theoretical concern, a mild pang, an accountable fact of the young.

It must have happened, he thought, when he handed over the money. He had dropped the coins and they had scattered down the promenade in all directions. Like the shard of glass, he thought, an accident on that day, at that time. The silver shards of money had slipped through his fingers. It took him minutes to retrieve all the coins. Having picked the coins up he had then flirted with the Polish kiosk girl who had wrapped the ice-cream cone in a napkin and smiled in that open way which any man would respond to and any woman feel vaguely threatened by.

He had then turned and started to walk back. And that

was when he'd seen that the wall was now empty. That was the moment the nightmare he now lived in had begun.

Shock, he thought afterwards, was a sacred thing. It hadn't felt like shock – for wasn't that what shock was, a denial of reality? It felt more like suspended animation, as if, believe it or not, he was coping.

Hoping she had returned home on her own, he followed her back, began looking in cupboards, underneath beds, in an insane game of hide-and-seek. He seemed to be functioning, but once removed, and it was only much later he realized he had not been *compos mentis* at all. He had only been going through the motions which took him inevitably onto the next moment of his life.

Olivia came home as he was shouting at the police down the phone, demanding that they help him. When the police had arrived Will had not screamed in their faces, fearful of alienating them. Fear and shock had made him impotent. He still remembered, all these years on, the look on the detective's face, that pale waspish face with thin lips and sudden understanding smile. A smile that actually didn't understand anything at all. 'She's just run away. She'll be back,' he had said to him. Oh, Will had hated the policeman in that moment; with the irrationality of terror he had hated him more than the abductor.

Afterwards he would relive those hours when he and Olivia had watched dumbstruck as the police told them not to worry, she would be found, and it was like a nightmare where there is no mouth where your mouth should be, only skin, and you are trying to speak or cry out and you can't.

Everything they were doing to get the police to act was done through a wall of pain. Even their movements and speech had slowed down, become sluggish. In that brief interval of time where something might have been done, he and his wife had failed Emily.

And those whom they had trusted to act on their behalf in a crisis had failed to take them seriously. The police had failed to take forensic evidence, failed to follow up the sighting of a strange man Will had seen hovering in the vicinity, failed to take witness statements. The police's failure was a different kind of failure: institutional failure, the failure of not caring.

And as the day progressed into night, it was as if time had malformed, become a different physical property altogether. Time stretched out in a vacuum: like solid air it went neither backwards nor forwards. Will simply existed within it. He didn't even feel as if he were waiting. He existed, he breathed this new dimension of time.

Detectives finally found the driver of a van who had been in the area: a young man with panicked eyes and thin mouth, with a criminal record for petty thieving. They kept him overnight but they had found no forensic evidence in his van to link him to Emily, no hair of her head, nor scale of her skin, nor drop of her blood.

It was like voodoo, he thought: if they could just find one atom of her, they could somehow conjure her up, the whole of Emily. That she might already be dead he could not even contemplate. The horror in his heart was like a huge darkness that swallowed up the future.

Chapter 13

The police had narrowed it down to the man Will had seen walking away – walking oddly, Will had noticed, as if his limbs weren't co-ordinated. No one else had noticed a man walking strangely and Will wondered if he had put on this gait to disguise who he was.

Will had the recurring image of this man walking away from him, and sometimes in his vision he would see his face clearly but it was always a different face. But always the same eyes: watchful, focused, almost beautiful.

And then the man would turn round again and start to walk away and William would make to chase him, to run after him – but would find he was unable to lift his feet, they were stuck to the earth. He collapsed to the ground, his legs as weak as sand, and watched this man who held the answer to what had happened to Emily walk away from him.

Will was haunted by this stranger, amazed that someone could hold all his emotions in the palm of his hand. Dwelling on what might have happened to Emily, his thoughts came to a stop, would not go beyond the brick wall that protected him from the information.

Will had knocked on the doors of the neighbouring houses, made criminal checks on recorded paedophiles – those who lived nearby and far away – but had not managed to connect them to the scene of the crime. Will and Olivia had also made pleas on the radio, not caring that their emotion had become sick entertainment for strangers. One female DJ shocked them by saying, 'It's probably better that she's dead,' but he was more shocked by his secret unspoken response: yes, it probably is.

And Will dreamt about catching the man with the odd gait but in the dream he does not give Will any answers. So Will takes him down to a basement. There is a concrete floor and a single bare light bulb hanging on a wire cord: the paraphernalia of a torture room full of hard edges in a hard light. And Will throws the man down on the chair. In the dream he is strangely compliant, as if Will's thoughts are driving the abductor's actions. *And they are.* The man's eyes look wide open, like a baby's caught in a flashlight. No one has ever looked more expressive and innocent.

Will takes out the rope from his pocket as if all this has been premeditated. He suddenly realizes he has planned this for weeks. He ties the man's hands behind the chair. He notices they are white and narrow with long fingers, a pianist's hands, hands that can play delicate music. He pulls the cord tight so he can see the rope dig into the flesh, the flesh rising up around the rope. The man lets out an angry sound.

'This is just the beginning of the story,' Will says. He is surprised by how his voice sounds in the dream, stronger and deeper than usual. Something is speaking through him: his own sense of justice. 'You have to tell me where she is.'

But the man remains mute.

Will is aware of time running out – Emily is suffocating or starving somewhere while he holds his captor here, trapped in this small room. He had thought just the threat of torture would make him speak, but he is just mumbling to himself now, crying and saying he is innocent.

Will knows what to do. He has never tortured before, never contemplated it: the word has only existed in heinous crimes, personal, international or political. The word doesn't belong to his own life. But he now knows exactly what to do. The life of Emily is at stake and he will do anything to find her again. To rescue her from pain, to bring her back into his life. As he takes out his pen, he can see her eyes in front of him, feel her arms around him, her soft hair brushing against his cheeks, the smell of her marshmallow scent.

The pen he uses is an ordinary biro. The type of pen you can buy at a newsagent for pence. Blue. It could have been any colour – blue, green, black or even red. But it is blue. He takes off the top and places the pen tip downwards over the abductor's left eye. The abductor shuts his eyes, squeezing them tightly. As if, like a child, he can will the world outside away.

'Open your eyes,' Will commands.

~

Portobello was where his soul lay and was also where the minutiae of the case – the clues – lay. Here, too, there was a sea-and-sky-filled response to the quiet gravity of his life. When the body of Mikael was washed up on the shore, the sea was returning to the town its own.

Will was always amazed what he could find on the shore. The detritus of other people's lives: condoms, pieces of map, pages from a comic, a baby's dummy. He had once even found a set of false teeth. At first the body, lying face-down, had looked like a log, blending in with the sand, but it was the wrong shape for the buried driftwood or plastic containers that were sometimes washed up on the shore. This was another kind of detritus: human life as detritus.

Will picked up the heavy cold arm to try and find a pulse. He turned the body over. Mikael's sensual face with his eyelids shut and long dark hair looked far more poetic in death than in life. Like a death mask in a museum, he looked as if all his questions had been answered and it had taken death to answer them.

At first Will could see no marks or bruises, but as he bent down he noticed a fine hole just behind his left ear, a small red circle as if someone had spiked his skull with a long thin instrument like a skewer. Looking again more closely at his face, Will saw blood had congealed just below his eyelids. He prised the eyelids open. Mikael's eyes were missing.

Will then noticed that something white had been stuffed between Mikael's teeth. Pulling open his stiff jaw, Will carefully extricated the damp paper from his mouth and smoothed it flat. It was a handwritten sheet from a diary, dated a few weeks before Louise went missing. It was a torn page from Lucy Verver's stolen diary. Will buried his head in his hands. So this is where her diary had ended up. In the mouth of a dead amusement arcade worker. This murderer liked playing games, Will thought. He also liked to join up the dots.

Will could just make out Lucy's faded words on the page.

Louise used to be practically mute. Now that her memory is coming back she's speaking gibberish. The other day she just said – apropos of nothing – 'I hope he finds me.' When I asked who on earth she was talking about, she replied, as if I were an idiot, 'Mr Sandman, of course.' The girl is clearly loopy.

Will was beginning to feel toyed with. He waited for the police to arrive and then returned home. In spite of the discovery of two bodies, Louise Verver was still missing, either dead, kidnapped or living happily in the country somewhere. And all he could see were loops and concentric circles of blood and loss.

He looked over at the jigsaw. This case was like the jigsaw, he thought: different disconnecting colours, some similar shades, and when was the grey the sky and when was it the sea?

Chapter 14

The following evening he climbed up the narrow steps to Granny's Attic, his legs heavy. Part of him seemed to be saying *walk away, walk away from here*: the same part of him that knew he was walking into danger. His personal life was quiet and self-contained, he didn't need to cross any line. He had a level of contentment and repetition to his days that were precious to him. It was all a matter of choice.

He could be vulnerable to obsession, he knew that. He knew that if he met the person who matched his own sense of loss, he'd be in trouble. But for years he had kept this thought imprisoned in its own private dungeon.

He feared involvement in the case too. There seemed to be, at the heart of it, a story about memory, people having trouble with their memories ... there was someone out there capturing, stealing their memories, memories that could diffuse into thin air like the souls of the dead.

The singer came onto the stage. As she started to sing, her voice seemed to reach into his deepest dreams in a way he couldn't comprehend. He was immune to women, he had thought, or rather immune to the love he had once felt for them. What was it about the singer that had such a strong effect on him? Was it the way she moved and smiled, as if everything was an echo of what he already knew, his unconscious conjured up, a dream come true?

As he watched her, he realized he had no idea who she really was, but this version of her had bewitched him like a spell in a fairy tale. He had begun to believe in her world rather than in his. The only reality was his desire. When he looked at her pale skin, he could see nothing beyond his longing for her – her face, her hands, her body. The reality of her struck him so forcibly because the reality of her flesh and bone was what he desired.

Her youth beguiled him and her youth seemed interminably connected with Emily, in some primitive, incestuous way. How could he distinguish the love he felt for his daughter and his desire for the singer? Love was so complex, so full of darkness and light, altruism and erotic selfishness, kindness and cruelty and sometimes obscure, illegible, slanted words. And the component of love seemed to consist of this confusion. The most simple, pure form of love was only the visible side, he thought. There was always the other side to love.

Will felt the room began to revolve. I have to leave, he thought, get out, but he was powerless over the feelings that triggered the electrical storm in his brain.

~

Will regained consciousness in the singer's dressing room. He could hear still her singing on the stage.

Sandman, I'm so alone
Don't have nobody to call my own
Please turn on your magic beam
Mister Sandman, bring me a dream

The words of her body, the metaphors of her soul, the similes of her scents, were like an imaginary novel he was reading, tricking him into believing that the desires that made us human and fragile were absolute. He knew he could still, at any moment, rip up this novel, reduce it to its separate parts until his dream lay in tatters on the floor.

He lifted his head. He was lying alone on a hard narrow bed with a seashell pink coverlet on it, in what looked to be a stage set for a dressing room. A sequinned dress had been flung over the back of a wooden chair. Jars of cosmetics, a mobile phone, contact-lens cleaner and blue-coloured contact lenses were scattered over the dressing table.

Will staggered to his feet. He had a pulsating headache. The light in the room was painfully bright. There was a bottle of water on the floor by the dressing table and he took a long, cool drink from it. The dressing table was backed by a huge mirror framed all around with light bulbs. Personal photos had been inserted around the edge of the mirror. They were mainly recent photos of the singer on stage or relaxing backstage in a state of déshabillé.

But there was one photo that was different from the others, that stood out. Will felt a sudden acute pain in his heart, as if it had been pierced by a shard of mirror. It was a picture of a young girl feeding a grey squirrel in the Botanical Gardens. She looked like Emily. It looked like one of the photos Olivia had taken of Emily a few months before she went missing. He remembered how his flat had been broken into and old photographs scattered across the floor. Had this one been taken from his flat?

The girl's face was obscured by the trees' shadows but her clothes, the way she was crouching... Didn't Emily once have a green tee-shirt and dark trousers like that? He carefully slid the photo out of the mirror frame and turned it over. Imprinted on the back was the date, over fifteen years ago, which made the girl in the photo the right age for Emily.

He slipped the photo carefully back into the frame of the mirror. The girl was wearing Emily's clothes, the girl looked like her, her physique was the same, but surely there were many other girls who looked like her? I'm going mad, he thought. He wasn't thinking clearly. His fits often left him muddle-headed. I have to resist this.

The singing had stopped and he heard clapping. The second part of the show must have finished. He lay back down on the narrow bed and shut his eyes. A few moments later he heard the soft rustling of a dress and the abrupt clicking of high heels as the singer entered her dressing-room. He kept his eyes shut as she bent down over him – he could hear her hard breathing, smell her mixture of animal and perfumed scent. Then he heard her walk over to the dressing table and dial her mobile phone.

'Yes. They found a body.' Her voice sounded as musical when she spoke as when she sang. 'Thank God you got the DVD to me quickly. He must have found out Mikael had been stealing them. I don't think he's traced it back to me... Yes, you just see the room. But I don't know where it is. Mikael of course wouldn't tell me. I'm sure he knew. And now it's too late to find out. But I recognize the room. I know I do... I can't say any more. I've got a punter here. He collapsed during the show. Speak to you soon, sweetheart.'

Will pretended to regain consciousness by moaning, and sitting up in the bed. The singer was leaning against the dressing table, a hand on her hip. He could still see what he had at first thought was the photo of Emily in the mirror just behind her.

'Are you all right?' she asked.

She didn't look concerned but the mask-like quality of her make-up and the distraction of her heavy platinum hair made her difficult to read. Her blue eyes were cool and appraising. She was going to be difficult to charm, he thought.

'Fine. I must have blacked out.' He didn't explain these fits were a regular occurrence, he never did. He didn't want people thinking him mad. Especially not her.

'It can get hot in here. And the flashing lights.'

'Yeah. That must have been it.' He would have to wait, be patient. As if he were fishing.

'Here, have this.' She poured a vodka from the bottle on her dressing table into a little toothpaste tumbler. The tumbler had a picture of a fairground Ferris wheel on it. He stood up from the bed and knocked it back,the pleasant sensation of burning in his throat helping him think more clearly.

'I'm just sorry I missed your performance.'

When she smiled it changed her whole face, made her look vulnerable like a young girl, but then the smile quickly vanished from her face like a phantom.

'You didn't miss much. The usual numbers,' she said drily. Why did he get the feeling she knew who he was? Had she remembered Mikael's warning about a private detective asking questions?

'I've got a bit of a sore throat at the moment,' she said.

'You'd never guess it.'

She looked at him strangely. Not too much flattery, he thought.

'So you've always sung?'

Her eyelashes flickered.

'I've always been musical.'

Her voice had a slight American drawl, which he hadn't noticed at first. She didn't have an accent when she sang.

'I'm from Chicago. The windy city.'

'That's what they call Edinburgh.'

She laughed. 'There's not much difference. And you have your own mafia now.'

The Russian mafia had come into Portobello in the past decade, bringing drugs and a small protection racket. She was sailing close to the wind bringing up the Russian mafia, with her connection to Mikael, Will thought.

'They don't bother you?' he asked.

'Only when they want something. Like most men.'

Will wondered how much Mikael had bothered her.

'I don't want anything from you,' Will said.

'It seems to me you might want everything.'

She smiled at him and handed him his coat. As he put it on, he casually walked over to the dressing table. He noticed a phone number written on a scrap of paper, lying next to her mobile phone. He recognized the number as Adam Verver's. Was it Adam she had just been talking to on the phone, or someone else in his flat?

Will gestured to the photo of the girl who was feeding the squirrel.

'Who's that?'

She didn't turn to look at it.

'Oh, just someone I used to know.'

How could he have thought the photo was Emily?

She walked to the door. She gave him an objective look but her eyes wavered just for a second. He now felt sure she knew who he was, or at least realized he was a detective. As she shut the door, he caught the look of wariness on her face.

Will left Granny's Attic with his heart pounding. The Louise Verver case was becoming inextricably linked with the singer. If he continued with it he would soon be at a point where he no longer had a choice, he would be dropping through the air, the ground moving at speed towards him. But for now he was still on the narrow edge just before the vertiginous drop, still in the part of the Venn diagram where sanity and insanity converged. He knew he could still step back, walk away. He had to protect himself from seeing her, thinking about her, wanting to touch her.

He woke up the next morning thinking *what am I doing*? A feeling of vacuousness overwhelmed him; his longing was pointless – a desire leading inevitably to disillusionment. When had desire not? – it was a sham, a hologram, an unreality of the subtlest, most potent form. Desire led your imagination, like a many-headed serpent, to branch out into the sky.

~

He phoned Olivia, feeling relieved to hear her clear voice on the other end. Talking to him she could immediately sense his general confusion about the case. But her insightful nature also served to heighten Will's general distrust of her objectivity. For, in their search for Emily, her icy perceptiveness had got them nowhere.

'Drop it, William,' she said. 'Don't go back. This case is taking you back, isn't it? To when Emily disappeared. This case is haunted, leave it alone.'

'I think I've just seen a photo of Emily,' he said, but even as he said it, he sounded insane.

'Don't be ridiculous.'

And he realized how close to the edge of madness he had grown, thinking that the back of a girl – any girl – could have been Emily.

Olivia had been clear-headed from the beginning. Soon after Emily's disappearance, he had caught sight of her reading a book, late at night, downstairs in the kitchen. She had looked utterly at peace with herself, as if Emily had not gone or never existed.

But Olivia's pragmatism became an impenetrable wall erected against him, a wall that no matter how hard he tried he could not break down. Or even climb over. Each brick of pragmatism was a little block of resistance against him loving her. He knew, though, that it was a façade, an elaborate façade. Even she didn't know what lay behind it.

Will was different. It wasn't a question, after Emily had gone, of him being remotely similar to how he had been. He had broken in two. But was *failure* – it sounded like frailty, it sounded like surety – such a terrible word?

Emily's absence in the house had choked him. He couldn't sleep at night, as if the empty bed in Emily's bedroom was of such unnaturalness it defied physical law. Lying awake at night, he had been transported to an alien world where the normal laws of probability no longer applied. It was a terrible new science-fiction world. The fits and visions that came later confirmed reality's uncertainty.

'She is alive, Will,' Olivia was saying to him over the phone. 'We just have to be patient.'

'How do you know?' he shouted at her. 'How do you know?'

'Will,' she simply said. 'Will, Will, Will.'

And she put down the phone.

Chapter 15

He had not expected to see the singer walking ahead of him, her pale hair falling down her back, as he took a walk along the promenade in the late afternoon. She was simply dressed in a pale grey shift; her only accessories were her bare skin and bones. From the back she looked like a young girl but he could see the swell of her hips and breasts. As soon as he saw her, he was again, in spite of himself, overcome by a hopeless longing. His imagination had collided with reality in the form of her body before him. But the fantasy of her was the stronger; it blocked out the reality of her physical presence until she became an echo of who she was.

He wanted to reach out and put his hand through his dream – even when she turned and saw him and spoke, he still couldn't believe it wasn't his dream speaking.

'Hello.' She smiled. 'Still not wanting anything from me?'

'Not yet,' he replied.

'Would you like to buy me a drink at the Milton, then?'

As they walked into the pub, Sean smiled at Will from behind the bar as if he had been expecting him. The Milton's pub was a large room overlooking the promenade and the sea. It had the usual strange atmosphere of a pub in the afternoon, like an empty stage set. Light gleamed through the window, shining onto the mahogany chairs and tables, giving them a lustre that made the room emptier than it already was. The afternoon light emptied the room of meaning, made it not so much insignificant as unenterable.

The singer crossed her legs and suddenly the physical reality of her swept over him and he saw her smooth calves and narrow ankles as if for the first time. Her stockings had a pearly sheen on them, like the mother of pearl shells he and Emily had once picked up from the beach, half-buried in the sand. He quickly looked up at her face. Her eyes were smiling at him. She leant over and for a moment he thought she was going to take his hand or touch him.

'You should bring pleasure back into your life.'

'Back?' He was defensive; how much did she know about him? She knew nothing, surely.

'It's been gone a long time. I can tell by the set of your mouth.'

'And I suppose you know pleasure personally?'

'It comes my way,' she said in her soft drawl.

In the fading light from the window he tried to see the reality of her face below the artfully applied make-up. Her face certainly looked different in this light, seemed more diffuse than on stage. It seemed she could read him but he couldn't read her at all.

A waitress brought them their drinks. Will was feeling awkward – this young woman was making him feel awkward. She still had that odd smile on her face. He had to remind himself of the case. He had to clear his head. The whisky was helping him.

'You're a detective, aren't you?'

'How can you tell?'

'It's in your eyes.'

He smiled. The feeling she had know all along who he was hadn't gone away.

'What, a kind of watchful, assimilating look?'

'A kind of dead look.'

He decided to move on quickly. 'I'm looking for a missing woman. Louise Verver.' He looked at her hard for a reaction but she was just staring at him interestedly. 'She lived in the block of luxury flats on the promenade. She hung out at the arcade.' He showed her Louise's photograph.

'I've seen her around,' she said. 'Always on her own. Wouldn't have thought she was married. She didn't look tied down to anyone.'

'At a loose end?'

'No, I mean free as a bird. As if she didn't have a home to go to.'

'Well, she certainly doesn't have a home now. We can't find her anywhere.'

He paused. 'Actually, I saw a friend of hers a few days ago in your dressing room. A boy, Miles Elliot.'

The singer looked amazed. 'How long have you been spying on me?'

'For quite a while. What was in the package?'

'Just something to watch.' She looked as if she were telling the truth: her face was steady, her eyes open, but her voice, normally soft and insistent, hardened. It was like the melodious tune of a thrush that had suddenly changed to a warning note. Then she laughed out loud, an almost hysterical laugh. She seemed to live in the present, shifting with each moment. He was stuck in the past; it was the present that was a foreign land.

It was getting darker, the light was falling. Will found the time when the light darkened sensual – that shifting again, that falling of light. When the light changed to darkness it meant other things were possible.

'The trouble with your profession is you're all *soooo* suspicious. You don't believe what's in front of your eyes.'

And at that point she looked at him so intensely he had to summon all his strength to hold her gaze. Oh, he believed what was in front of his eyes all right. Sitting there in the darkness, the candlelight flickering around her, the sky still not dark, just a dark blue, he had never believed in reality so much.

'It will never be possible, you know.'

'What do you mean?'

'You know what I mean.'

Desire had become for William about the transgressive. The girl was so much younger than him. He wanted her youth for himself. It wasn't her innocence he wanted – she was not innocent – it was her distance from him. When he looked at her it was like looking back through time.

'I'll be in contact with you, if I need you again,' he said.

'You can always reach me at Granny's Attic.'

He put money for the bill on the table and left the singer looking out at the darkening sea.

On the promenade it was an icy night and the lighthouse was throwing its beam across the sea. It was like a scene from another world except for the sound of his feet on the concrete. Seeing the earth's shadow on the moon, seeing the moon glow blood-red gave him a cruel perspective, turned his heart cold.

Will knew his obsession with the singer was connected with his tendency to melancholy: two sides to the same impermeable, glittering coin. A coin that he wanted to throw into a wishing well and walk away from, leaving it shining under the water for someone else to pick up.

He came to the oracle at the west end of the promenade. The oracle never closed down, the light bulb in the box was always switched on. He put his money into the priestess' outstretched hand and then wrote clearly on the card that popped out of the box, *Who is the murderer?*

A few minutes later, after a whirring of internal machinery, the oracle churned out its answer:

You are.

Chapter 16

He needed to find out what was in the package Mikael had given the singer. He made a few phone calls to a friend in the police force and found out Mikael's address – he'd lived in a small flat overlooking the river in one of the poorest areas of Leith.

An old parking cone and some litter were floating in the water outside the tenement block where Mikael had once stayed. Will climbed up the communal worn stone steps which smelt of bleach and urine. A young woman with the hollow eyes of the drug addict, carrying a child's buggy under one arm, pushed past him down the stairs. Mikael's room was on the top floor; the door had been boarded up by the police and appeared padlocked. As Will examined the padlock, the clasp unlocked in his hands – somebody had already picked it open.

Will entered the flat. It was a mess – whether it had been ransacked or whether Mikael was just very untidy, Will couldn't tell. He guessed it was a combination of the two. The small spare room had been used as a darkroom; there were trays full of liquid, smelling of strong chemicals. The living room was full of photography equipment. Rows of DVD boxes marked *Arcade* lined the shelves. All these boxes were empty. The DVDs had been taken away, presumably by the person who had broken in before him, probably Mikael's and Lucy Verver's murderer.

Had the murderer found out that Mikael had been stealing these DVDs from the arcade – what was on them? The singer had mentioned a room – and then selling them on for money?

Will went into the bedroom; all over the walls were plastered photos of Mikael in different disguises: in Arab dress wearing a heavy beard, fakely tanned in a swimming costume, a gold medallion hanging round his neck. He obviously fancied himself as an artist.

Will tried to work out how he could tell they were all so clearly the same man. It was the way he held himself, he thought. His head projected just slightly forward, his shoulders hunched, no matter what the disguise. And he had the same watchful eyes, whether as a Mormon or a disco king.

But one of the photographs stood out as different from the rest – it was a smaller Polaroid, rather than one of the larger more formal pictures, and unlike the others had been pinned haphazardly to the wall. It seemed to have been added to the collection like an afterthought. Will went over to look at it more closely. It was a picture of Mikael sitting tied to a chair in a brightly lit basement room. Blood was pouring from his eyes. Someone had taken a photograph of Mikael being tortured and then pinned it up on the dead man's wall.

~

The next morning, Will drove into town to the handsome registry office at the East End of Edinburgh where the statue of Wellington reared up on a horse outside the front door. Will walked down the large imposing corridors to the central office where the birth and marriage certificates were held on computer databases. He looked up Louise Verver. He could find no record of her birth – nor any record of her marriage to Adam.

Returning along the promenade to his flat, Will saw the blind man coming towards him. He walked as if he had no fear, as if there were fewer obstacles in front of him than in front of those who could see.

'So, Will,' the blind young man asked, 'any luck in finding the mysterious disappearing woman? I expect she still doesn't know whether she wants you to find her.'

Will was surprised by his choice of words; they reminded him of the oracle. If indeed his visions of Louise had been real sightings of her, she certainly had been acting in an ambiguous way, as if she were taunting him with her appearances and then disappearing again. As if she wanted him to find her and didn't at the same time. Was this some elaborate game that she was playing or the torturous charade of an amnesiac?

'But she's never met me.'

The blind man laughed, the deep laughter that comes from realizing the world shares your sense of humour.

'Are you sure?'

'So you've talked to her!'

'The woman who I heard arguing with her husband? Oh, yes. In the days before she went missing she became very talkative. She began to say very interesting things.'

'Like what?'

His eyes looked more intense than usual, more blue. Will wondered for a mad moment if he *was* blind.

'That the detective who had his offices on the promenade was one of the few people who could help her. She just had a feeling about your name. She would also say funny things

100

like how wrong it is to steal someone's childhood away. And that people are not who you think they are. "You can't trust anyone," she repeated, "anyone." She was also remembering things she thought she had forgotten forever. She remembered on her childhood bedroom wall a picture of the Mad Hatter from *Alice in Wonderland*.'

'That was a common picture,' Will said.

~

The conversation with the blind man had disturbed Will and he went home to write down the main points of what had happened so far: Louise Verver going missing, Belle sending the blackmail photos to Adam, the murder of Lucy and Mikael, Belle visiting Olivia's gallery office and the DVD from the arcade given to the singer. He couldn't get the points to connect, to make sense. Perhaps they didn't, he thought; perhaps they were simply incidental to something else.

Late that afternoon he took another walk on the promenade. It always helped to clear his mind, the combination of walking and fresh air and the brutal nature of the sea. He approached the oracle and was just about to ask it a question when he felt the terrible dizziness and pressing headache that presaged a vision.

There in front of him stood a six-year-old Emily, wearing a pinafore dress and brown jumper, looking very serious. She was standing absolutely still, like a statue. He slowly approached her. As if in a dream, he was overjoyed to see her again but did not find it strange she hadn't aged.

'Daddy,' she said.

'Emily, where have you been?'

'I've been here all along, Daddy. You just didn't notice.'

'I would have noticed. It's my job to notice. As your father, I would have noticed.'

'No, Daddy, I was right under your eyes and you just didn't see me.'

'What about your mummy?'

She gave a wry smile. 'Oh, Mummy never notices anything. We know that, don't we?'

'But you're not being clear. You mean you're in Portobello?'

'Playing on the beach and everything.'

'I'm so sorry I didn't see you.'

'That's all right.' Emily lifted up her arms to hug him and as he embraced her she dissolved in his grasp.

He recovered his senses. The promenade was empty; two children, warmly wrapped up, were playing on the beach. A child scooted past. He still had a headache. He staggered over to the oracle and part of him felt like crying. These visions were physically and emotionally draining, as if the exertion they demanded from him was a work of art in itself, or a labour of love.

The oracle on the promenade was waiting as always for a question but he realised it had to be the right question. Still stunned from his vision of Emily he wrote, *Will I ever find Emily alive?* and inserted the card into the bottom slot. The whirring began and a few minutes later out popped the card: *Only after you find out she's dead.*

'You're a charlatan – a charlatan machine!' he shouted, and he kicked the machine until his foot was sore.

Chapter 17

He rang the bell to Adam Verver's flat and heard Miles' quiet voice telling him to come up. Miles was sitting at the computer in the spare room, his pale skin looking as if it had not been in the sun for many years. It was as if he were living in a dungeon. Will felt sorry for the boy; his instinct was to help him if he could.

'Where's Adam?' Will asked.

The boy shrugged his shoulders. 'I wouldn't worry about her, you know.'

'Who?'

'Louise, who else?'

'Why not?'

'She likes to do her own thing – when she went to the amusement arcade, it wasn't really to play the machines.'

'What do you mean?'

'The gambling was an excuse for her real compulsion. To keep returning to the arcade.'

'Why the arcade?'

'She didn't know. She just said she couldn't stop herself going there. It was something to do with her past. The memories that were coming back involved a room in the arcade.'

'Did she tell anyone else this?' Louise Verver had clearly been in a highly confused state of mind.

'I don't know. I don't think so – it's not something you would mention.'

'No,' Will said. 'I don't suppose it is.'

As the boy turned to his game again, Will couldn't resist saying, 'Reality can be quite interesting too, you know.'

'Yeah,' the boy replied, 'but is it fun?'

Will looked into Miles' eyes; they were a lustrous green and they gazed back as if nothing in the real world could hold surprises for him any more.

'Like a rollercoaster…' Will said.

Will looked down at the boy's computer screen. On the screen were grainy images of a young woman or girl sitting on a bed, reading, then getting up and stretching, then turning on the TV. The image was unclear and obscure.

'What is that you're looking at?' he asked.

'Oh, it's just a girl.'

'What do you mean?'

'It's private.'

He shut the screen off.

'Do you know her?'

'Only on the screen – how can I? It's like she's mute.' Miles looked up with his empty eyes – like glass eyes, Will thought, like the apparently seeing eyes of the blind man.

And this world on the internet, full of different networks, odd connections – was this some sexual game the computer boy was playing? At Miles's age, a hard new sexuality had coursed through Will's veins and made him who he was. But Miles seemed asexual. Then again, Will had known men – the apparently asexual ones – who had hidden their sexuality away, locked it up until it had become powerful and distorted. Their placidity had become a mask brought about by years of secret practice.

He noticed the boy exited the site via *Oracle* but his attention was distracted by the screen saver picture: it was a recent photograph of Will's room. His desk, bookshelves, the globe in the corner... He suddenly felt cold. There was no sign of pieces of jigsaw on the table; the photo must have been taken before the jigsaw arrived.

'Where did you get that picture?'

The boy looked surprised by the urgency of his voice.

'It's just a picture of a room.'

'Yeah, I see that. But where did you get it?'

'I found it.'

'Where?'

'It was just lying on Louise's desk.'

This case increasingly seemed to be implicating him. The blind man had told him Louise believed Will could help her – this was before he was assigned to the case, before she went missing. He had been trying to look at it as if it were a separate reality, and instead it had become a reflection in a mirror that was hanging in his house.

He remembered the break-in of his flat, the discarded camera wrapping-paper in his bin. Had Louise broken into his flat, just to take a picture of his room for her computer screen? And then another thought struck him. Was it Louise also who had sent him the jigsaw afterwards?

He turned his attention back to Miles. 'It seems a weird picture for you to choose.'

'I like to imagine the person living in it.'

'And what kind of person is that?'

'Oh, someone lonely, someone lost in the computer game of life.'

'Like you,' Will pointed out.

For the first time, the boy smiled.

'Actually, like you. You're looking tired.'

Will left the boy sitting in front of his computer, feeling in some way obscured. The various identities, the confusion of memories, the shifting sands of relationships made Will wonder if he would have to begin acting according to his own laws.

He quickly glanced around the penthouse's empty living room. A vase of crimson roses had been placed on the glass coffee table next to a pile of magazines with names such as *Computer World* and *Technology Today*. On one of the covers dated a few days before Adam had first visited him, Adam had scribbled, *Ring Blake about Louise's disappearance. I like to tempt fate…*

Lying in bed that night Will felt a cold drop of water land on his face. He looked up. Rain was beginning to drip through the ceiling. He moved his pillow to the other end of the bed, away from the leak, and perched a bucket on the bed at the other end, beside his feet. He listened for a while to the soft drip, drip of the water falling into the plastic bucket before finally falling asleep.

Chapter 18

The Chinese girl was on the beach feeding the seagulls and he joined her as the birds fluttered and squawked above their heads.

'You look tired, Mr William.'

'People have been saying that a lot recently.'

He felt tiredness had become imbued in him like age, an inevitable decline of the physical body.

'Do you sleep well at night?' She looked at him quizzically.

'On and off. Can I have some bread for the birds?'

She gave him some bread. If you can't beat them join them, he thought bitterly. The seagulls were now screeching like banshees.

'I'm on a difficult case. A missing woman.'

'If she wants to be found, she will.'

'Is that an ancient Chinese proverb?'

'No, just an observation. Sometimes I go missing for an hour or two, away from home, if Mum gets cross with me. But then I will return to the place outside the café until they can spot me and call me in for tea.'

'This situation is a bit different.'

'You need someone to look after you, Mr William. You work too hard.'

'You are so right,' he replied. 'But having someone would just complicate things.'

She shrugged her shoulders matter-of-factly. She was so different from Emily, he thought, with her pragmatic hardness. He loved her for being so different from Emily, was grateful. There was no way this exquisite little dark-haired girl with her ochre skin and self-contained manner could ever have been Emily. She was no reminder or pale echo.

'You, Mr William,' she said, 'should just get a grip on reality.'

He laughed.

'Every day I do exactly that. It's my job, reality – I wrestle with it, as I would a huge grey elephant; it has a trunk and clumsy feet and flapping ears. Believe me, I see reality wherever I go. It would be impossible to miss such a huge hulking beast.'

'There used to be an elephant in the old arcade at Portobello,' she said. 'A hundred year ago. It was my school project. There was also a tribe of African tribesmen on show. For visitors who paid to see them.'

'See, what did I tell you? Reality is everywhere.'

~

Like a *deus ex machina*, Olivia phoned from the Portrait Gallery.

'Will, I'd like to see you as soon as possible. Can you meet me tonight?'

'Sure.' He never questioned her.

'I'll meet you at the George Hotel.'

The George was a luxurious Edinburgh hotel in George Street at the heart of the New Town, a place of chintz and clinking teacups. As he entered, he saw Olivia reclining on a plush floral sofa in the reception area. Sitting next to her was a man he had never seen before. As she noticed Will, a rare look of anxiety swept over her hard features. It was gone in an instant. Will slouched down in a plush floral chair opposite them.

'Will, this is Graham.'

He nodded, looked at Graham, and managed a smile. He was handsome and well-dressed with fair Nordic features: the opposite of Will. Will didn't feel anything. He was surprised by his lack of jealousy. Was he the man who had given Olivia her garnet ring?

'It's not what you're thinking.'

'No?'

'No. Graham thinks he may have a clue about Emily.'

The sound of a seashell in his ear, the distant roar of the sea. I must keep in control, he thought, not lose consciousness.

'Are you feeling all right?'

He nodded. Even Olivia didn't know about his fits. He didn't want pity.

'You look feverish.'

'These hotels, with their central heating so high. Their guests must be cold-blooded.'

He glanced at Graham. Graham looked bored, as if forced here against his wishes – but presumably he had come of his own free will.

Graham started to speak but Olivia interrupted him.

'You do understand this might not be infallible, William?'

He nodded impatiently, 'Yes, yes.'

He looked at Graham hard; he had never waited so hard for anything.

'I remember thinking I had seen her before.' Graham

paused. 'I must have seen her on television. So that's why I recognized her.'

'Yes.'

'I had travelled to Switzerland for a job interview.'

'When?'

'Soon after she had gone missing.'

'Where did you see her, exactly?' Will felt like someone else was asking these questions, anyone else but him.

'Geneva. In a restaurant.'

'Alone?'

'No, she was with a woman.' A woman was involved in this, he thought.

'What did the woman look like?'

'I couldn't see.'

'How was she? How was Emily?'

'She looked happy.'

She looked happy. Emily looked happy. He didn't know whether to laugh or cry.

'And you were sure it was Emily?'

'Not definitely. All I can say is it looked very like her.'

'And why are you telling us now?'

'I only returned to Britain a few months ago. I wasn't absolutely sure it was Emily. Then a friend mentioned they knew Olivia. I felt I had to tell you.'

Will was used to the frailty of witnesses, their reluctance to come forward, as if they were afraid of seeming foolish. It was the ones who were eager to come forward, attention-seekers, the amateur detectives, who were often mistaken. There was something in his uncertainty that made Will think Graham had indeed seen her in Geneva. But so many years ago.

'What was the name of the restaurant?'

'I'm sorry, I can't remember.'

Olivia was looking at William with soft eyes. 'She has been taken by people who wanted to adopt her, a normal family.'

'Perhaps,' Will said. He felt faint. 'Would you excuse me? I have to leave. This is incredible news. I need time to think about it.'

Will ran out of the hotel in such bewilderment that he left his coat behind. As he returned to the reception room, he saw Olivia hand something over to Graham. Will waited a moment and then walked up to them.

'Forgot this,' he said, picking up his coat.

Will waited in a nearby lane with a clear view of the hotel front entrance. Five minutes later Graham came out and disappeared round the corner down a cobbled street. Will followed him down the street and grabbed him from behind, holding him tightly in an elbow lock.

'What did she just give you?' he hissed.

Will pulled out an envelope from Graham's inside jacket pocket and ripped it open; inside was a wad of notes. He spilled the money onto the ground.

'What's this for?'

Graham just stared at him.

'You never saw her in Switzerland, did you? Olivia just paid you to say this. Why?'

Will now had his hands around his neck and was practically choking him. Will relaxed his hold. Coughing, Graham replied,

'She wanted to put your mind at rest. That Emily was safe and happy. And perhaps being looked after by a loving family. She wanted to put your mind at rest.'

'So she paid you to tell me a pack of lies. How could she

do this? How could she be so stupid? If there's one thing I'd never thought Olivia, it was stupid.'

'She seemed desperate.'

'What do you mean?'

'She said she thought you were on the edge of a breakdown. Seeing photos and thinking they were of Emily.'

Will gestured at the money on the ground. 'Take it. You probably thought you were doing me a favour.'

Graham walked quickly away, shaking his head, leaving the money on the ground. A sudden gust of wind blew the notes down to the end of the lane where Emily was standing, her arms outstretched towards her father.

'Daddy, I can hear the sea.'

'But we're in the middle of the New Town. It's the traffic.'

'No, I can hear the sea.'

Chapter 19

The next morning Will sat down on a bench a hundred yards down the promenade from Lord Verver's house and waited. Ten minutes later he saw Miles coming out of the house. Will followed the boy at a distance to a bus stop on the High Street and then onto the bus. Miles climbed the steps to the top deck and Will stayed on the lower. The anticipation he felt when following someone was located on the surface of his body, like the low level hum of electricity.

Miles got off the bus at Craigmillar. Craigmillar was one of the poorest areas in Edinburgh, a council estate built in the 1930s to replace the slums of the Old Town. 1960s high-rise flats surrounded it. Will followed Miles past the boarded-up houses and the shops with metal shutters to keep out the drug addicts.

Miles had an odd walk, robotic, as if his joints had stiffened up. His face had a sad passive look, as if it could soak up any world event or major incident with equanimity. Litter lay profuse on the street: newspaper, sweet paper, pornography, paper of all kinds except literature. Syringes lay in the gutter. The industrial site was a block of warehouses just beyond the wasteland at the centre of the estate. Miles crossed the grass that was littered with patches of dog excrement and ignored a desultory group of boys playing football.

Will watched as Miles disappeared into a warehouse

with FUTURE PRODUCTIONS painted in large, wobbly, unfuturistic writing on the side of the wall. He wondered about Adam's brilliance; this warehouse seemed gimcrack, not the result of a radical scientific genius.

A few minutes later Will followed Miles in. He found himself in a large, dimly lit concrete room: cardboard boxes were piled up high and the floor was stained with a rust-coloured substance. The place smelt of sawdust and rubber.

'Hello,' Will called out. He could hear the sound of children playing outside on the wasteland. He suddenly felt disconcerted. He walked further into the room.

'Is anyone there?'

He noticed the boxes were all marked with the word *Future* and he went over to one, but they were sealed shut. He looked around and still saw no one; he ripped one of the lids open. Inside the boxes were what looked like small component parts for computer chips, tiny black pieces with wires sticking out like caterpillar legs. Will sifted the loose black components through his fingers. Machines with memories, humans who acted like machines. Had the person who had taken Emily felt like a machine? he wondered. Metallic sharp edges, with mechanical momentum and an inability to feel another's pain.

Emily had once fallen from a tree and come into the house, blood pouring from a gashed wound in her forehead. He and Olivia had been sitting in the drawing room when Emily ran into them.

'Get off the carpet, Emily,' Olivia had said calmly. 'Blood's seeping into it.'

Sure enough, blood was staining the cream carpet. Will had seen that Emily was white with shock, hardly able to breathe, let alone cry. As Olivia had bent down to look at the stain, he had picked Emily up and carried her down to the nearby doctor's clinic. She had needed a few stitches but he had been equally shocked by Olivia's uncaring reaction. It had not been natural, he thought, more like a machine, and as the black plastic innocuous components shifted through his fingers like sand, he thought of Olivia and her automatic, stylish irreversible ways.

Just then he heard murmuring coming from a small room at the back of the warehouse. Through the opaque glass door, he could just make out Miles and the figure of a slim woman with fair hair. She was saying, 'I'll be leaving soon, Miles. I just wanted to thank you for helping me so much. And to say good-bye.' A moment later Miles came out of the room, tears streaming down his face, and caught sight of Will.

'What are you doing here?' Miles asked crossly. 'Have you been following me?'

'I thought you might lead me to Louise.'

'Well, you're not going to find her here.'

The boy was blocking the door to the back room. 'Who were you talking to?' Will demanded.

He pushed him aside, but it was too late: the room was empty and the window the woman must have crawled out of was too small for Will to squeeze through. By the time Will had run through the warehouse to the front door she had disappeared.

~

The computer shop was full of technology, bleeping and blinking. The man at the counter was young, with dark hair falling over his pretty features.

'I wonder if you could tell me what this is.' Will handed over some of the components he had found in the warehouse.

The man looked at it carefully.

'It's a component for a webcam. But it's like nothing I've seen before. It seems very sophisticated. The retina seems more like a human eye than a machine. It can swivel. It actually looks like a human eye.'

Will looked at it lying in the palm of his hand. It looked nothing like an eye to him. It looked like a small, flat, dark grey piece of silicon.

'Thank you.'

'Where did you get it?' the young man asked – he looked curious, intelligent.

'Oh, I can't tell you. It wouldn't make any sense…'

~

Adam phoned.

'Any developments?' Will could hear the desperation in Adam's voice. Will was sure that he had no idea where Louise was.

'Nothing definite. I'm following various leads.'

'Well, let's hope one of them takes you somewhere.'

Will mentioned nothing to Adam of his visit to Future Productions or Miles's secret meeting with a woman. The woman could have been either the singer or Louise – Miles seemed linked to them both. Nor did he ask the scientist about the sophisticated surveillance equipment that was in his company's warehouse. Having reassured Adam that things were progressing, Will put down the phone, feeling uneasy. Under Adam's sardonic tone, Will had sensed fear. Not fear for his missing wife but fear about something else. What was Adam scared about?

~

There was one house at the far end of Portobello that stood in the middle of wasteland beneath a giant electricity pylon, as if everywhere around it had been destroyed in an apocalyptic attack and for some fairy-tale reason it had remained standing.

It was a handsome three-storey Georgian house, full-square with steps leading up to the dilapidated front door. Occasionally, Will would notice a light going on behind drawn curtains but he never saw anyone coming or leaving.

An attempt had been made to cultivate a small fenced garden amongst the wasteland covered in old washing machines, bits of bike and decrepit computers, and the house and garden seemed to Will against all the odds to transcend its surroundings.

Boys would come at night to smoke drugs in the darkness outwith the garden, using the junk as furniture, their joints or heroin foils flickering in the dark, the pylon guarding them like a giant sentinel. This house was where Will had once lived.

William had not returned to the marital home since the break-up of his marriage. He would just go and observe it from time to time. He often wondered why Olivia hadn't simply sold up and left. A chi-chi flat in the New Town nearer her work would have suited her far better. Staying here, she was forced to commute at least half an hour into the centre of Edinburgh.

Nor did she ever use the promenade. Since Emily had gone

missing she had never gone back there. Everything about the place, she had told him, had reminded her of Emily's absence, from the empty arches of the amusement arcade to the melancholy of the deserted beach. It was the only sign that Emily's disappearance had affected Olivia in any way.

Will wanted to search the house. He wanted to find out the real reason why Olivia had tried to persuade him that Emily was living safely in Switzerland. He used the old house key he still kept on his ring to open the door. Inside, the house was strangely minimal with white-painted floors and walls and the occasional piece of modernist furniture. She had emptied their home of its clutter of antiques and prints.

He searched the house but could find nothing of relevance. However, he did notice there were security cameras in every room. Olivia must have felt that living alone, surrounded by the council estate with its drug addicts and steel-shuttered shops, was like living in the middle of a war zone. Will felt ill-at-ease with the changes she had made; the place seemed oddly inhuman, inexpressive as the geometric precision of a piece of machinery.

He returned to the living room – the separating wall that had once divided two rooms had been knocked down by Olivia to create a larger, lighter single room with white linen sofas and white rugs. All this white was giving him a headache. It was like snow-blindness. An unfinished chess game stood on the table.

He looked through her DVDs, mostly art documentaries which were all clearly marked. But one DVD, dated a month ago, caught his eye. He picked it up. An attempt had been made to erase the label on the box. It was only because he had seen similar DVDs in Mikael's flat that he could just make out the faint imprint of the word *Arcade* written on it.

He slipped it into the DVD machine. There was the image from what looked to be a webcam of a young girl sitting cross-legged on the bed in a room filled with technological goods. She was naked.

Chapter 20

Will went back to the Milton and asked Sean when Belle was on. Sean gave him a knowing smile.

'She's on now.'

As Will climbed up the stairs he didn't know what he was thinking. He wasn't thinking at all. There was no answer when he knocked on the door, so he just opened it.

In spite of the sun outside, it was dark inside her room. A red scarf had been flung over the lampshade to give the luminous red glow of sex. Belle was lying on the bed. The sophistication, the creamed finish of her had gone. Her make-up was lurid; she looked transformed. It occurred to him that this whole case seemed to be about confused identity. People looking like each other or different from themselves; people who were missing and people who were not.

She was sprawled across the bed in transparent black lingerie, clearly high on drugs. He understood the attraction of drugs, that dulling of reality. It changed your perception. It was like finding a religion: a religion that came in material form. Drugs were dead reliable, as long as you could get hold of them. He looked at the photo of Jade again and wondered if Belle still thought about her missing daughter.

He handed her the money. He wondered how he was going to get a prostitute who was high on drugs to talk.

'What can I do for you?' She sounded surprisingly lucid.

She must be iron-willed, he thought.

'I need some information.'

'I normally keep it to myself. But I'll make an exception for you.' She gave a leery smile.

'So I'm getting special treatment?'

'You could say that.'

'Why?'

'I don't like to see people getting confused.'

'And I'm confused?'

'It looks that way. Rose tells me a detective has been asking about Louise Verver.'

'Yes, I'm trying to find out where she's gone.'

'Women go missing for different reasons. Mainly for our sanity. If we didn't go missing we'd go mad. It all gets too much,' she said. 'I go missing when I'm having sex with a punter I don't like. It's possible to go missing just for a few minutes.'

'What about going missing for weeks?'

'Her husband visited me sometimes.'

'Is that your explanation?'

'He had bad habits. Disgusting habits. He liked to pretend I was a young girl.'

'Louise wasn't on the game?'

'Not that I know of.'

Prostitutes generally disappeared for the same reason: psychopaths. And they did not disappear for long; their bodies would soon turn up on wasteland or dumped in a canal, dismembered or mutilated. The disappearance of a prostitute meant the presence of evil. He didn't know what the disappearance of Louise Verver signified.

'My daughter went missing,' Belle said quietly. 'A while

121

ago. No one gives a fuck.'

'Did you go to the police?'

'Are you crazy? I'd just get into trouble. They'd say she'd done a runner.'

He remembered his own experience. 'When did you last see her?'

'Louise Verver?' She looked hard. 'Actually, the last time I saw her, she was with a man I'd never seen before.'

'Where was this?'

'Just outside Granny's Attic.'

'What did he look like?'

'Odd-looking. Dark. Wearing a trilby. '

'Mikael from the arcade wore a trilby. Are you sure it wasn't him?'

'Positive.'

'Does this guy even exist?'

'I'm not making him up. He was very conspicuous. One of the things I noticed was that he had an umbrella. I thought that looked odd.'

'Why?'

She looked at him as if he were very dense. 'Because it wasn't raining.'

'Did it look like it might?'

'The sun had been out all morning.'

'Well, you know Scottish weather.'

She shrugged her shoulders. 'It seemed put-on, if you know what I mean.'

'I do… How were they together?'

She paused, then met his eyes directly.

'Lovey-dovey…' She said it so softly he could hardly hear her. 'He was holding her tightly, kissing her.'

'It wasn't Adam Verver?'

'Nothing like him.'

'How was she with him?'

'Very responsive.' She kept eye contact, her drugged eyes unassailable.

'Can you remember the day?'

'It would have been a few weeks ago. I remember 'cos I had a sore throat.'

'So, around about the time she went missing.'

'If you say so.'

'And there was no sense of coercion at all? No feeling she was threatened in any way?'

'I told you. None at all. She looked the happiest I've ever seen her.'

Her story sounded fabricated. Why was Belle making all this up? Who was she protecting? He turned and quickly looked around the room. Lying on a side table was a laminated membership card for a health club, New Life. The name *Adam Verver* was clearly printed on it. He quickly looked away.

'It looks like you could do with some love,' Belle whispered.

'Well, a little bird tells me you've been meeting my ex-wife for coffee.'

For the first time in their conversation Belle looked anxious.

'And I didn't think you were the jealous type. She's an attractive woman. Can I get you a drink?'

She quickly poured him a whisky into a glass. He downed it in a single gulp. It didn't taste good.

'Aren't you having one?' he asked.

'I don't drink during the day.'

The room was misting over, the red light growing redder. She was now looking at him strangely. He was not sure exactly when her suggestive smile had turned into an expression of seriousness. His whole mouth tasted bitter. He staggered into the side of her bed. Instead of asking him what the matter was she just stared at him, as if waiting for something to happen.

Will regained consciousness flat-out on a wooden floor. He had a mind-altering headache and his limbs felt heavy. Light was pouring through the skylight in the roof. He judged it to be morning light. He must have spent the night there. Beneath him, on the floor below, he could hear an irregular clicking sound. He clenched and unclenched his hands – the skin was unbruised. He hadn't been tied up.

He was lying in a room used for storage: empty cardboard boxes lay around and empty filing cabinets stood forlornly against the walls. He gingerly staggered to his feet. The metal triangular roof looked vaguely familiar. He checked his pockets – his wallet was still there. He tried the door; it was unlocked.

Cautiously he opened it; he went outside and found himself on a balcony. He could hear murmuring below and looked down to see a few old-age pensioners playing bowls on the green baize floor of the local indoor bowling centre. The clicking he had heard upstairs had been the sound of the bowling balls striking each other.

Finding a back stairs, he descended to the second floor where there was a café overlooking the sea. As he reached into his pocket for change to buy a strong coffee, he pulled out a Polaroid photo that had been slipped into his pocket.

The photo was of himself lying unconscious on the floor.

He had been blindfolded. A note had been placed on his chest saying, *Leave this case alone.* It seemed that Belle liked to leave notes for people. For Adam, for Olivia, and now for him.

The danger surrounding this case had encircled him. He was at its epicentre. He was interested in missing people, he cared. That's why he was good, and it had led him to this. For some reason Belle didn't want him to find Louise Verver.

~

He looked at the jigsaw lying on his table at home. A picture was beginning to emerge of a wall, part of a brick wall: the side of some kind of building. The pieces were tiny and it was inevitably time-consuming: even after a solid hour of working on it, he had only managed another few square inches. Will had also picked out a few black jigsaw pieces that looked like fragments of lettering.

His eyes were beginning to feel strained and he took a gulp of whisky. A sensation of emptiness overcame him, like dropping down a well, this weird sensation of falling through darkness, as if his heart had dropped inside him.

What was he doing in this life, he thought, a lone man with a lost daughter and an ex-wife, in a rented flat in a decaying seaside resort, working with the low-life – he was that detritus too. But then he rallied – he was still alive, he had not gone missing – *although some part of him had*.

He went to sleep and had deep strong dreams of running through streets at night, deserted neon-lit streets, turning corner after corner, not sure whether he was chasing someone or running away but feeling the breeze of a hot summer's night on his cheek.

Chapter 21

Will could no longer stop fantasising about the singer. Oh, but this fantasy was good to him, it treated him well, it thrilled and excited him. He felt his skin becoming more sensitive, as if being touched. The fantasy was starting to consume him as he knew it would, as he was asking it to do. For weren't feelings the most real thing of all? Even misguided ones based on a mirage. He had built up his own figment out of these thoughts and emotions and they were as real to him as the beach, the sea, and the hard unforgiving stone of the promenade. But he knew his obsession's dark side too. Its consuming power. Its lack of humanity. He was falling apart, the outer demeanour of his personality flaking off.

He kept on returning to Granny's Attic but the singer was never there. One evening, disappointed again by her absence, he was drinking there when he noticed a girl sitting in the corner. It was Emily. He approached her.

'You are drinking orange juice, aren't you?'

She nodded. 'Of course, Daddy; I'm only six.'

He sat down beside her.

'Emily, I've come to say that I have been looking for you for years. You haven't changed at all.'

'You look older, Daddy.'

'Where have you been?'

'I've been here all the time, Dad, just round the corner.'

He kissed her on the top of her head, just to check she was real. He could smell her hair.

'But where? I've searched here, everywhere.'

She looked at him with steely brown eyes that shifted between melancholy and laughter in a second.

He had loved her volatility. Emotions floated over Emily like shifting images from a projector on a blank wall. Her expressiveness made her body fluid – unlike the repressed emotion that occasionally stiffened Olivia into an elegant but stultified pose. He had once thought it feminine but now thought it cruel.

'In a labyrinth,' Emily replied.

On returning home he poured himself a whisky. He wondered about the exact definition of a labyrinth and took out a dictionary.

Complicated irregular structure with many passages, hard to find way through without guidance, maze, intricate or torturous arrangement; entangled state of affairs.

The next morning he started work on the jigsaw again. The different colours were starting to form specific images: the silver of a sword held by a young man, the dark red hair of a beautiful girl, the grey face of a dying woman. The colours told the story of Elektra. The same story that was pictured above the entrance of the arcade.

He looked again at the package that had contained the jigsaw. The writing was in heavy anonymous capitals, slanted imperceptibly backwards – someone who was left-handed, perhaps. Emily had been left-handed. She had got it from her mother who was left-handed too.

~

Will drove north down the coast until he saw a pinnacle of shiny steel-laced flats rising up to the sky like the skyscrapers of Dubai. There was huge development taking place here on the old docks, harbours replaced by expensive apartments for city workers who could commute into the centre of Edinburgh. The pale yellow brick building of the health club New Life had been built on the water's edge.

At the entrance of the club the turnstile stuck. The receptionist, a young woman made up like a china doll with a careful manner, said, 'Have you got a membership card?'

He smiled. 'Do I look like I have a membership card?'

She looked at his slightly stooping posture and pale complexion. 'I'm afraid it's a strictly members-only policy.'

'Oh, I see. Like a prison, but in a good way. I'm a private investigator.' He showed her his card.

The girl looked taken aback.

'Oh. Well then,' and she pressed a button behind her desk and the turnstile opened.

Will walked down a spacious marble corridor which opened up into a large open-plan room with a café on one side and seats in front of a large pane of glass on the other. Beyond the glass were tennis courts. One court was being used by young children but it was the two players on the other court that caught his eye.

He felt suddenly transported to another reality. For the tall loping man on one side of the net was Adam. And on the other side, concentrating and beautiful, Olivia. His eyes bore down on them for any hint of chemistry but he could find nothing. If anything, they looked slightly bored. But then

Adam Verver said something and Olivia burst into laughter.

He thought he had come to grips with the ordinary reality of his daily life, a reality of gentle contours and gradual permutations but this tableau between his wife – no, ex-wife – and Adam was a reality of a different order. A new, awful, vivid reality that made his previous world a place of shimmering shadows.

His mind struggled to make sense of what was happening in front of him. Why had neither of them mentioned they knew each other? His brain scrambled for an explanation, a rational innocent one. Perhaps it was coincidence. He had mentioned neither of them to each other. Neither had been told of the other's connection to him.

He tried to remember what he had said to Olivia about the case, if he had revealed any names. He didn't think he had. He was sure he had never discussed anything of his personal life with Adam. He hadn't even mentioned he'd been married. So what were the two of them doing here together, playing tennis?

Chapter 22

He stopped Olivia in the doorway of the health club after Adam had left.

She turned on him. 'What are you doing here?' she hissed. 'Following me? Like a common criminal? Leave me alone, can't you?'

He had never seen Olivia look so intense; her pale eyes looked like the wild sea. What was happening to her, what was Adam doing to her? Although Will had managed to eradicate most of the love he had once felt for Olivia, a residue remained, like salt on the body after swimming in the sea. A trace of salt crystals that were slightly abrasive to the skin.

'How long have you been seeing him?'

Her eyes fell to the ground.

'It started when we were still married, a few months before Emily went missing. I couldn't fight what I felt for him, Will; I tried, believe me.'

Will felt as if the wall that Olivia had built between them was falling down brick by brick. And landing on his head. To reveal another Olivia. An Olivia who deceived. She had been so clever – but there was never any doubt that Olivia was clever. He just hadn't guessed at her hidden emotions.

The clues he had prided himself on spotting in his detective work, he had missed in his own home. He had been blind to what was closest to him. Her loss of desire for him had

had nothing to do with Emily. It wasn't that she hadn't been passionate, she just hadn't been passionate for him.

'How long did it last?' He couldn't bear to look at her. He remembered how she had grown more distant, more inaccessible in the final year of their marriage. How he had put it down to her work.

'Just six months. I only started seeing him again recently. Don't be jealous.'

He didn't reply. Jealousy was an inevitable part of love. It was a component, a natural component. He didn't believe love was rational or light or all-forgiving; love was primitive and dark.

'What made you start seeing him again? *After fifteen years?*'

She hesitated, only for a second. 'After he abruptly ended it, I never stopped thinking about him.'

When she had first met Adam all those years ago, it had come out of the blue. She had been visiting an exhibition in the Modern Art Gallery with Emily. He had bumped into her, had held her arm for a moment. It was an innocuous but very deliberate act, like the grasp of a demanding child, an act of pure will. He held her arm for too long. And she found that urgency, that straightforward demand from this adult man, impossible to argue with. They had talked for a while about art; he had given her his card.

Afterwards she wondered why she had been so compelled by this initial meeting. Was it to do with his intelligence or his stillness, as if asking her to take all the meaning she liked from him?

She didn't know this man. She had no idea about his kindness but she wasn't interested in kindness. She was looking for a connection – an experience as real as the contentment of her married life, just a different reality.

The next day, she had picked up the phone and slowly dialled his number, feeling nauseous. She let it ring once. Then she put down the phone. She couldn't do it, it was impossible. No, that was the trouble: it was possible, but she wouldn't do it. That settles it, she thought; the thought of him would settle like dust under the bed. But she knew part of her wanted to rewrite her present life, make it dangerous and unpredictable.

She was sure the initial reciprocity of desire would end in her floundering. Unless, of course, he could sustain her desire, be equal to it. And that she would never now know, never let herself find out. And when she put down the phone, she was also putting the phone down on her ever knowing.

It was just a moment; that was what she came back to, a moment. She knew nothing about him, about his history, what exactly he was looking for. But how could she have ever known when finally she rang him what he was really looking for?

~

On the screen the girl looked about seven but the picture was unclear and Miles couldn't make out her face. She was certainly wearing young clothes: jeans and a tee-shirt. She was looking straight at the camera. It reminded him of the room on the DVD he had given to the singer. He had played it quickly before giving it to her.

As he now looked at the screen, it didn't occur to him to come to the girl's rescue. That would happen in the real world. She was in the cyberworld, where connections only happened through cyberspace. Coming to her rescue would like be trying to rescue a heroine from a soap opera on television. This wasn't reality. Miles leant back in the chair. He hadn't felt so real and in his own skin for as long as he could remember. He went to bed and dreamt of the meadows and streams he had once played in.

Chapter 23

Portobello could be a reflection of Will's moods. It seemed to have all the emotions: hope, despair, excitement and dullness, according to the weather or the time of day. Sometimes when he spoke to the oracle it seemed that Portobello conjured *him* up, with a twist and a sigh of its folded hands.

Will returned to the oracle. The priestess had a sign hanging round her neck saying *Closed for the foreseeable future.* The slot for the questions and replies had been masked by black tape. He felt like smashing the oracle into pieces, because even this had been taken away from him, a gimcrack mysticism that bordered the promenade and gave him hope he was not alone in his search for truth.

Often as he looked around he saw that others were not interested in truth at all, that they led their lives according to quotidian needs and desires. He, William, was obsessed by truth. He had believed it existed and that the oracle was not an old machine on a dirty promenade but the last semblance of reality. He kicked it and let out a yelp as another sharp pain went through his foot.

'What are you doing, Will?' It was the cool young laconic voice of Lily. 'It's only a machine.'

'When did they shut it down?'

'This morning. I saw them come.'

'Who?'

'Two men. In yellow jackets with *Edinburgh Council* written on them.'

'Do you know why?'

'Apparently it broke down. It kept giving people the same message.'

'And what was that?' He began rubbing his foot. The pain was only gradually going away.

Lily brought out a neatly folded piece of card and unfolded it.

'It kept on repeating the same message for days. People were demanding their money back from the arcade.'

Will looked down on the card. On it was written, *Memento Mori.* Will couldn't help laughing. It was so typical, so oracular, so incongruous with Portobello.

'Why are you laughing?' Lily looked slightly offended. 'It's true, isn't it?'

Will looked down at his large muscular hands. They looked invulnerable but women had kissed them.

'I don't know,' he said. 'I've still to find out.'

'Will.'

He looked at her.

'You are too hard on yourself.'

'Someone has to be.'

He walked out onto the promenade. The seagulls let out their familiar cry, which made him nostalgic and afraid at the same time.

That evening he went round to Granny's Attic. He sat down on a seat that smelt of musk and sex and bought a whisky from a friendlier Nancy. She had finally forgiven him. The whisky's hot sweetness condemned him to a different state of mind.

He was ready to resist the most voluptuous of feelings until the singer came out onto the stage wearing a taupe wrapped silk dress that was a few shades darker than her pale skin. He had never seen her look more erotic, as if everything but desire had been stripped away from her face. She seemed to be offering herself up to all possibilities.

She had a suggestiveness that reminded him of his detecting. For his work was a series of suggestions that he followed through: possibilities, alternative realities. Nothing was certain until he reached the end of the case – and sometimes not even then. Her hair was tied back to reveal her oval face; her eyes looked darker – brown, not blue – more liquid than usual and her lips seemed fuller.

She sang as if he were the only person in the room. The old man in the corner and two younger men at another table seemed more involved with their drinks than looking at her. But William, although he had seen much, had not seen this before: this song sung in this particular way by this person. He felt as if the present had been given back to him. Having lived for a long while in the past, time had shifted to the acute experience of now. A sensation he had forgotten about and had thought he would never have again.

The combination of the whisky, the music, and her sensuality threatened to overwhelm him. A misty light descended and the architecture of the room seemed to withdraw into the shadows. He felt a fit coming on, and for the first time, instead of fighting it, he gave into the sensation. As the emotional intensity of the moment passed, so did the feelings of vertigo.

He watched her move her body to the music, swaying

slightly with her hips and arms, as if she were not dancing but letting the music infuse her blood. And for a moment she was no longer human but made up of notes and melody and longing. She was liquid, translucent song and he was not so much listening as watching her voice made incarnate. The singer invited him to imagine her.

Later she joined him for a drink at one of the tables. She sat down beside him and he could smell her potent scent. Everything about her was glittering. Everything about her made him forget the mundane details of his life. When he looked into her hazel eyes he saw her future ahead of him. And he struggled to see himself there too with her, and couldn't. But her mouth was smiling at him, half-open, and he bent over and kissed her and realized that his future didn't matter.

He then took her hand and held it; it looked like a small replica of his.

'You should look to Olivia,' she simply whispered.

He was astounded. 'What do you know about Olivia?'

She smiled. 'Olivia is responsible. It's all her fault.'

Her words chilled Will. 'What's all her fault?'

She buried her head in her hands, then looked up, distressed. 'Sometimes, you know, I don't know what I'm saying. The words come out of nowhere. I only hope one day, you can love me in the way I need.'

And she stood up and walked out of the room. What did she mean, love her in the way she needed? What did she mean that the words came out of nowhere? This infatuation was depleting him, asking for more than he could ever give, asking him for more than was humanly possible – it was a parasite, feeding off the blood of its host.

~

Belle was looking up at him from her bed, clear-eyed and undrugged and naked. He looked at her breasts, her narrow waist and wide hips, a configuration of irresistibility. Will loved the tousled look of women in bed. They spent so much time grooming themselves, he often thought the pleasure was in the dismantling of their appearance, the shedding of artifice, piece by piece. Belle, with all the wiles of her profession, would know this; after all, prostitutes were expert in the sexuality of men, their peccadillos, their sins. Prostitutes knew about their fantasies and needs. That was why men went to them. They knew about suggestions, if that was what you wanted. And that was always what Will wanted.

'I've missed you, William.'

'You have a strange way of showing it.'

'I had to drug you.'

'To warn me off the case. Why?'

'I don't trust the law.'

'I'm outside the law.'

'You're a detective, aren't you?'

'It's just a word they call me.' He paused. 'What are you afraid of?'

'Jade,' she said. 'I'm frightened of what will happen to Jade if you get involved.'

'What has the girl got to do with the Louise Verver case?'

'I can't say any more.'

'How is Olivia involved?'

'Adam used to talk to me about Olivia.'

'I've seen them play tennis together.'

'That's not all they do together.'

'I know.'

'Adam would speak about her often. And how your daughter went missing…'

And she looked defiant, moving her hands to her hips, her dark eyes flashing. Her body offered itself up as a challenge to him: take pleasure from me, if you dare. He knew the prostitutes who put on their act, went through the charade of pleasing or dominating, while their eyes flashed red and green like traffic lights.

Chapter 24

Will walked into the hall of the National Portrait Gallery and looked around. What had the singer meant, that Olivia was responsible, that it was all her fault? The singer was like the oracle, he thought. She seemed to utter these words as if she didn't know where they were coming from, as if they were welling up from her unconscious in spite of herself.

Will hadn't told Olivia he was coming. He saw her, standing with her back to him, looking up at the sweeping mural, in gold gilt and luminous colours, of the figures of Mary Queen of Scots, John Knox and David Hume. He was just about to approach her when he saw Adam enter the building. Will ducked out of sight behind a large sculpture.

Olivia and Adam kissed and then Will followed them up the stairs into one of the empty galleries off the second floor. He watched as they sat down together on a bench in the centre of the room, surrounded by Raeburn's bravura portraits of philosophers and generals in their heavy gilt wood frames. The flocked red damask wall covering gave a dense backdrop to Olivia and Adam, as if they were other portraits come alive in the room. Will waited in the shadows of the door and began to listen.

'Mikael betrayed me,' Adam was whispering. 'He was stealing DVDs from the arcade. He sold one on to someone. I don't know to whom. He refused to tell me.'

'A DVD?'

'Like the one I sent you.'

'It was just film of a girl in a room. I don't understand.'

Surely Olivia could guess what it might signify, Will thought. It was not like her to be *faux naïf*. Olivia's obsession with Adam meant she was no longer in touch with reality.

'I'll tell you everything. When you're ready.' There was a sudden coldness to Adam's voice Will had not heard before.

'And your mother?' Olivia asked in a matter-of-fact tone. It was as if Olivia were in a trance, as if she could hardly believe what she was asking.

Will was starting to find it difficult to breathe. Everything he had thought he had known about the world since Emily had gone missing, had been shaken again. He saw the back of Emily's head running away from him into the distance. But her hair had turned platinum like the singer's.

'The scribbles in her diary – they'd become too revealing,' Adam said softly. Scribbles, Will now realized, that Adam had stuffed into Mikael's mouth after murdering him, too. Before he had thrown his body into the sea.

'And Louise?'

Will heard him hesitate, just for a second. 'Louise should have appreciated me ... Like you appreciate me.'

He brought Olivia forward and kissed her. A look close to madness had come into Olivia's eyes. Cold Olivia, Will thought; how he had not known her at all, and how utterly secretive she had been, how deceptive. Her infidelity and now this. Disgust crept into his heart like a rat crawling across a floor.

Adam took her hand. 'Don't you betray me now, will you, Olivia?'

141

~

The girl looked at the four walls around her. This was now her home. She had a television set and a bed and over the months she had gradually adapted to a room that was ten foot by ten. A poster of a map of Africa taken from a travel agency catalogue hung on the wall. She thought she always changed in privacy behind a screen until she noticed a camera in the ceiling above her there, too. And then she stopped bothering about privacy. After a while she forgot about the cameras altogether, just waited for the next meal or film to be delivered. Sometimes she felt as if she were in a video game herself.

There was a tiny slotted window far above her head and birds would sometimes perch on the sill there. She would watch their fluttering wings with eagerness, as the only natural movement in her room was herself. Everything else was technological; the moving slot in the DVD machine, the state-of-the-art television, and of course the revolving eyes of the cameras.

She had also become an expert at reading sounds. She could hear what the weather was like outside – windy or still. Sometimes she was sure she could hear the sea but then she wondered if it was the distant roaring of cars down a motorway. She missed the rain – the cold wet rain on her face and hands, the comfort of her mother roughly rubbing her hair dry with a towel.

The girl allowed images of her home into her mind like old photographs because they gave her feelings in a way that technological entertainment could only dream of. She accepted her fate with the phlegmatic nature of childhood. She had grown accustomed to a sense of bereftness. A solid absence that stood like a black stone monolith in the corner of her room.

She had not seen the face of her captor; he wore a mask. But he watched her, she knew, through the cameras positioned around the room. Their red lights never switched off. The cameras were his eyes. The cameras blinked ferociously like eyes. They were eyes. They worked on the same principle, with their mechanical retinas.

She tried to bring the natural world into this world of technology a bit at a time. She had been given video games to play that mimicked reality but what she really wanted were fragments of the real world. She would pick up crumbs of food and dust from the floor and make a shrine to these shards of physical reality. A large component of the dust was her own human skin that she had shed during the night.

She dreamt she constructed another human form to play with out of the human skin. In her dream she created a little girl just like her.

'I've made you. You have to do what I tell you,' she told the girl.

'I'm not your child,' the dream girl replied and stared at her. Her eyes frightened the human girl. 'But *you* are a child,' the dream girl continued, 'you are someone's child. Where are they? Where are your parents? Why aren't they looking for you?'

'Mum is,' the girl said. 'She is.'

'Then why hasn't she found you? She can't be trying hard enough. She's out of her head on drugs, isn't she?'

'She will find me,' the human girl said. 'It's just a matter of time. I know she will find me.'

And then the dream girl started to laugh and the girl noticed as she bent back her head and laughed that her teeth glinted metal. And that her sky-blue eyes were flickering red like the flickering of a camera. The dream girl's eyelids suddenly shut and opened like the lens shutter of a camera. The dream girl was taking photographs of her.

And she caught a glimpse of the dream girl's scalp behind her ear and saw it was hard and grey and shiny like metal. And then suddenly metal began bursting through her skin. And the girl realized she wasn't a version of her at all but an automaton in disguise. She was really an extension of the gadgetry in her room, part of her domestic dungeon, inhuman. And the human girl launched forward, bringing her to the floor, hitting her, pulling at her limbs until the metal girl lay in pieces on the floor.

On the days her jailor came in, he didn't speak. There would come a day, she thought, when she would no longer feel human. She would become a robotic girl like the girl in her dream, strong in the way machines are strong, durable and made of steel.

~

Will's sexual obsession with the singer had become an escape from his torturous thoughts, a metaphor for his despair. He kept on remembering how, after he had kissed her, the singer had held his glance for a few moments. Her dark eyes had looked at him as if she were searching for all that was good in him and all that was vulnerable to desire. It was as if she had read his mind, and this artful connection between the

144

mind and desire, he thought, was what made us human, was at the heart of our consciousness.

But now Emily was walking toward him. Six years old, a boyish irrepressible grin on her face. He took her in his arms, smelling apple on her face. Nothing was as soft as her hair, not the underbelly of a mouse, or the feather down of a three-day-old chick.

In his ear she whispered,

'Daddy, I've been here all the time. I never really left you.'

And he found himself saying,

'I know that, Emily. You've never been out of my head.'

And he fell down on the pavement feeling the bile in his mouth and the bitterness on his tongue. 'Emily, Emily, Emily' – an insane chorus ringing in his head.

Chapter 25

The following morning, Will was walking along the promenade when, as if out of a dream, he saw a woman with golden red hair appear ahead of him. He felt his body turn to clay. What was Olivia doing here? She'd told him she couldn't bear to return to the promenade since Emily had gone missing. Will had never thought to see her here again. It would be like returning to the scene of the crime. It was all wrong. The sea had changed to the colour of her hair.

Here Olivia was, walking down the promenade as if this place held no meaning for her at all, this place was merely a matter of geography, with no shadows or echoes. She was walking as if Emily wasn't present in every grain of sand, every wave that washed up on the shore. And Will's thoughts turned frantic. If Olivia was capable of forgiving Adam, what else was she capable of? Had she been involved in Emily's disappearance?

An overwhelming sense of nausea rose up in his chest and throat and Will leant over the promenade wall and threw up violently onto the sand, hurling up thin green bile. Shaking and shivering, he wiped his face with his sleeve, the taste of acrid vomit in his mouth.

The bond of parenthood was torturous, inexplicable and unforgiving. The love for a child didn't make sense, the self-sacrifice defied logic, it was not a moral love but an irrational connection. Could Olivia have broken that connection? She had deceived him once over her affair; what else had he failed to see in her? He started to follow her. It was a strangely similar day to the one on which Emily had gone missing.

He followed her, Olivia not once looking back. Her singular vision kept her moving forward into the future. Olivia was the opposite to the oracle, Will thought. She didn't want the future now, but kept at a safe distance, just a little bit ahead of her. She turned up the path into the Milton Hotel. In all the time they had lived in Portobello they had never gone there. Olivia's sense of decorum and taste would not have allowed her near a place like that. Olivia's standards had appeared high, he thought bitterly, until she had become involved with a psychopath.

He followed her into the hotel. She didn't go to the bar but made straight for the staircase. Will could no longer predict the direction of his thoughts. Had his ex-wife become a prostitute? Or was it simply that she had in *some way* become involved with one? He watched from the landing as she knocked on Belle's door – Belle visiting Olivia's office at the Portrait Gallery, now Olivia visiting Belle's place of work: two different worlds of fate, destiny, class, colliding.

Will saw Belle open the door and Olivia disappear inside. Soft murmuring started up from inside the room. He swiftly climbed the stairs and stood outside the door to listen. Just then he heard the sound of Rose's door opening and Rose appeared in the doorway. Her green eyes widened in surprise as she saw him standing there, her auburn hair falling in curls down the back of her trenchcoat. He was convinced she was going to shout out a warning to Belle. But she just smiled at him and whispered,

'Still waiting for her? You'll be waiting a long time…' and ran down the stairs.

The murmuring between the two women had grown more intense so he put his ear to the door.

'He's beginning to confess things to me. We're almost there. Adam's beginning to trust me,' Olivia was saying.

'He doesn't trust anyone. Be careful…'

'I will be… What about Will?'

'Don't you see, Olivia, we still can't tell him. We have to keep him out of it. And off the Louise Verver case. If Adam feels Will suspects him in any way, he'll panic.'

'You're right.'

'I can't thank you enough,' Belle said. 'For what you're doing.'

'I'm doing it for myself, too.'

'It's probably too late for Emily,' Belle said gently.

'Perhaps. I'm still hoping that if we find one girl, we find the other.'

He heard the two women embrace each other. Olivia let out a small moan of pleasure and Will quickly turned to go back down the stairs.

Olivia was innocent. He was shaking. He sat down on the promenade wall outside the hotel and buried his head in his hands. He started to sob, sob for his lost daughter, his lost marriage and lost dreams.

~

As he looked down at the jigsaw all Will could see were the spaces for the missing pieces, spaces that fitted the contours of Adam Verver's psychotic mind. And he dreamt that Adam

148

Verver's brain had missing spaces that matched the missing spaces of the jigsaw. For psychopaths were not complex. They had no imagination. They just had absence and their own desires.

He was woken up the next morning by the phone ringing.

'I want to call off the search.' It was Adam. Will tried to remain calm.

'You've found Louise?'

'No, but there's no point going on any further.'

'Why not?'

'I said I want to call off the search. Send me the bill.'

'All right,' Will said, and hung up.

He immediately walked down the promenade to Adam's flat and waited in a nearby doorway for him to leave. Then he ran a neighbour's bell.

'Who is it?' a querulous old lady asked over the intercom.

'Adam. I've locked myself out.'

She buzzed Will in without further questions and he climbed the stairs, his heart racing. He forced the lock on Adam's flat, not caring how much damage he did to the pristine white door. He entered, searched Adam's desk in the living room, but found nothing. The wastepaper bin was empty.

Will entered the spare room where Miles liked to play his computer games. Pulling out the main drawer of the desk, he found about twenty photographs of an empty room, all taken from different angles. There was a pile of girl's clothing in the corner, surrounded by technological gadgetry. On the back of the last photo was written: *Password – Echo*.

Will switched on Miles's computer and found the website for *Oracle*. He typed in the password: *Echo*. Up onto the screen appeared the same room that had been in the photos, and on the DVD in Olivia's flat. The absence of anyone in the room was palpable. It was like a postmodern work of art, about negation. It seemed to be about the person who wasn't there.

The bed had the narrow institutional shape of a prison bed. There was a screened-off area. And then he noticed the shoes: a small pair of shoes, about size one. There was no other sign to show the age or the gender of the person who lived there. Then, for the first time, he noticed a barely perceptible shape under the covers: the shape of a child, head buried under the blankets. It was Emily, he thought, it must be Emily. But it can't be. She would be older – but a madness overcame him and he became convinced it was her.

Chapter 26

The blind man stopped him on the promenade. 'I heard Adam Verver last night.'

'How do you know it was him?'

'He always tends to whistle the same tune: *The Magic Flute*.'

'He doesn't greet you?'

'Why should he? He doesn't know who I am.'

'You know who he is.'

The blind man simply looked at him.

'He was coming from the amusement arcade.'

'How do you know?'

'He smells of it – the carpet has a distinct smell.'

'Playing the machines?'

'I guess.' The blind man shrugged. 'But I didn't hear the sound of loose coins in his pocket. His clothes are always silent.'

'Always?'

'It's a regular trip for him to go to the arcade at night.'

'What time is this, generally?'

'After midnight.'

'The amusement arcade shuts at eleven.'

The blind man shrugged his shoulders again. 'You figure it out. Isn't that your job?'

Will continued on his walk. He found the dusk that night

particularly appealing, as if it were pulling him towards an answer. Dusk would pull him along like a puppet on a string, just as the unconscious pulls us toward our dreams.

Will found himself outside the flashing lights of the arcade. He looked up at the painted mural of Elektra that ran above the entrance of the arcade. He looked again at the black lettering of *Et in arcadia ego* above it – "even I am in Arcadia". The "I", Will knew, referred to Death.

Abba were playing *Money, Money, Money* again. Sometimes it would be *If I Were a Rich Man* from *Fiddler on the Roof*. The catchy melodies of Mammon. The singer sang songs in a minor key. There was contagious joy in the major but truth in the minor.

He entered the hall of the arcade, where the sinister clown beamed down at him, and climbed the narrow steps at the back, to the office on the top floor. The manager of the arcade looked pleased to see him.

'Hallo, Mr Blake. I haven't seen you in a while.'

Will sat down opposite him in the small pokey room. A print of Vettriano's *The Singing Butler* was hanging on the wall. 'I just wondered if you'd noticed anything unusual here recently?'

He laughed. 'Something unusual happens here every day of the year. Staff go AWOL. Strange noises at night. What kind of unusual do you mean?'

'Strange noises?'

He gave another laugh. 'It's just the whirring of the machines. Even though the cleaners are sure it's the sound of someone shouting.'

Will tried to fend off a devastating excitement rising in his body.

'Do you have a basement here?'

The manager looked at the detective strangely.

'Sure. We store the broken slot machines down there.'

'Can I see it?'

He took Will down through a fire exit, down linoleum-covered steps through another door into a large gloomy basement. Pieces of old machinery projected out of the shadows. Will could make out the high priestess of the oracle propped up against the wall, a detached arm lying by her sandalled feet. An insect buzz was emanating from a ventilation system. There was no one down there.

'Thank you very much.'

As he turned to leave the room, he caught sight of something on the floor. He picked up a small card on which was written *Memento Mori*. Will put it in his pocket.

This basement unnerved him. He had a final look around and could see no hidden door or trapdoors.

'And there's no other exit?'

'Nope. Just the door we came in by.'

Will followed the manager out. The arcade felt hot and stuffy compared to the cold darkness of the basement. Adam Verver visited the arcade regularly late at night, like Louise before him. Mikael had stolen DVDs from there. The picture on the jigsaw matched the outside mural. The DVD in Olivia's flat bore the faint traces of the word *Arcade*.

He came out into cool evening of the promenade. Lily was playing on the beach. He went over to her.

'If you were stuck in a room somewhere and couldn't get out, what would you do?'

'I'd try and escape.'

'And what if you couldn't?'

'I'd wait for someone to rescue me.'

'And what if no one did? What if no matter how hard they looked, they couldn't find you?'

'I would never give up hope.'

He looked at her. No – she was strong and resilient. But Emily? She had his mixture of strengths and weaknesses – different sides to the same coin. Sometimes his strength of will made him weak, other times his susceptibility gave him intuitive strength. But after years of imprisonment, what would have happened to Emily, cut off from reality and the reality of who she was?

He thought of her boredom, to exclude any other possibilities. Will depended on her boredom reaching out into every minute of the day until time seemed to go sideways. Boredom kept her safe from harm.

Chapter 27

Will waited outside the Portrait Gallery for Olivia to come out. To remain unseen he negated himself, so Olivia's attention would not be attracted to where he was standing behind a wall. She came out, stood on the doorstep for a moment and then turned left, walking briskly towards the West End, down one of the narrow lanes off George Street.

Will followed her to the doorway of a nearby shop. A half-naked mannequin looked down at him as if she had seen it all before. He watched as Olivia entered a small French restaurant. A few minutes later he watched Adam walk slowly down the lane and follow her in.

Through the window, Will could see the scientist join Olivia in an area partitioned off by a silk screen painted with a Japanese heron. Will realized he could enter the restaurant without their seeing him. He sat down on the other side of the screen and signalled to the waiter for a drink. He could hear what they were saying, even though they were speaking softly.

'I'm impressed,' Olivia said. Will immediately recognised the soft surrendering note of sexual infatuation. She was a good actress. She had acted for her husband during the last months of their marriage. She was now acting for her lover. 'How did you take her?'

'It was easy enough. After school. Jade had seen me often

with Belle. It was just a question of trust.'

Will was reminded of people's desire to confess, wanting people to bear witness to their truth.

'You seem so expert at it. As if you'd done it before.'

There was something slightly hesitant about Olivia's voice, as if she were not quite focusing on the present. Will prayed Adam wouldn't notice her distracted manner.

'The other girl was the same. She had met me a number of times already. One day I followed her and her father to the promenade. Her father left her alone for a few minutes to buy an ice-cream. I approached her. I told her that her mother had suddenly taken ill – that she had to come with me. It worked like a dream.'

'Emily!' Olivia's voice sounded awe-struck.

'You've known all along, really, haven't you, Olivia? That's why you came back to me. You're intrigued.'

'Emily was the reason you first approached me in the gallery, wasn't she? It was her you really wanted, not me.' Olivia was trying to sound jealous.

'I wanted you both.'

'You never hurt her?'

'Never. You must believe me, I loved her. Always treated her gently… You seem pale, my darling.'

'No, I'm fine. *But you're putting her in the past tense.*'

Adam hesitated for a moment. 'I've bad news, I'm afraid, Olivia. After about ten years, Emily tried to escape from the room where I kept her. I struggled with her. She banged her head. I rushed her to hospital. But her injury was too severe. She died.'

Will felt his whole world shatter into pieces, as if everything around him had broken into fragments. How was Olivia surviving this?

'Olivia, I'm sorry. It was an accident.'

'Yes,' Olivia said. 'Yes … of course … And Jade?' She breathed the name.

'She's in the same room I once kept Emily. But also on a website. A secret site within one of my games. For voyeurs. They like to watch a young girl in a room. It's a kind of reality show.'

Will saw in the reflection of the window Olivia stand up suddenly from the table, knocking her chair over. Adam looked startled.

'Adam, I'm sorry, I'm feeling a bit faint. I need to go outside for a moment.'

Olivia didn't see Will as she ran past him out of the restaurant.

Before Will could run after her, Adam suddenly appeared round the screen. It was as if he had been looking for Will, known he was there all the time.

'What are you doing here?' he asked. He looked so normal, Will thought, *such a respectable man*.

'How did you know I was here?' Will asked.

'I sensed someone listening through the screen.'

Adam had picked up on Will's emotional state – he had become conspicuous.

'Was our conversation interesting?' Adam asked Will.

'Oh, very.'

'Whatever you've heard, you will keep it to yourself, won't you? Olivia is feeling very fragile at the moment … We wouldn't want anything to happen to her.'

'Oh, don't worry, Adam, I won't tell anyone.'

Will rose to his feet and left Adam in the restaurant staring after him. He searched the nearby alleyways until he found Olivia cowering alone on some steps. Will sat down on the steps next to her.

'I could have helped you, Olivia.'

She didn't look at him, stared straight ahead as if communing with the shadows on the street. He gently turned her head towards him and looked into her grey eyes. He had never seen eyes so full of pain. 'When did you start to suspect him?' he asked quietly.

'I always wondered… But stupidly I put my suspicions down to guilt over our affair.'

'But Belle suspected him straightaway? Of taking Jade?'

'Yes. Adam had talked to her about me – and about Emily going missing. He likes to do that. Play games with people. Belle thought it was too much of a coincidence, him being connected to two missing girls. Realized he must have targeted us both for our daughters.'

'So she tried to blackmail him?'

'But the photos she sent him had no effect – Louise had already gone by then. Besides, he wasn't worried about a prostitute. A junkie prostitute. His word against hers. The police would never have believed her.'

'So Belle got in touch with you?' He took her hand in his.

'She thought I might be able to help in some way.' Will noticed that whenever Olivia spoke about Belle, her voice grew soft.

'But in *that* way? You went back to him knowing what he might have done?'

'Don't you see, Will? I had to. It was all my fault. It's because of me he met Emily. I let him into our lives.'

'You didn't know then, Olivia – you didn't know what

he was really like.'

'I was always sure we'd find Emily alive. Always. I had to be. And now she's dead.'

She hid her head on his shoulder and he held her tightly as she finally broke down.

~

Will went round to the promenade flat that evening and rang the intercom.

'I was expecting you,' Adam Verver said. 'Come on up.'

Will found him at his desk making notes. Adam looked up as he came in. His eyes were bright and shiny with light that came from within: the glare of the fanatic. But the small pupils took no light in.

'Look at you, Dr Verver,' Will said quietly. 'Working away on your AI projects. How much of a real scientist are you? Does *Echo* provide you with an income your genius can't give you?'

'You don't understand. I don't get support from the scientific establishment because my ideas are so radical.'

'What ideas, exactly? You don't have any ideas, do you? Geniuses are visionary. You don't have any imagination at all. Just your sophisticated surveillance machinery and paedophilia sites.'

'Why don't you get to the point?' Adam Verver asked.

'What have you done with Emily?'

'Unfortunately she died in hospital.'

'You're lying, you're lying!' Will screamed at him.

Adam sneered at him, 'What a clever detective you are.'

And William hit him. He struck out at Adam Verver. He

couldn't stop himself. He had never felt so clear-headed. It was the opposite to dreaming. He hit him as hard as he could across his face, chopped the back of his neck with the side of his hand, brought him to the floor. He struck him again and again in the face until he was a bloodied pulp, until he was unrecognisable and just a mess of flesh and bone.

'I've got her back,' Will shouted again and again, 'I've got her back,' as if the hitting of Adam Verver gave reality to the words, cemented the meaning in blood, that Emily had returned to him.

Will waited in the flat until nightfall, with only Adam's dead body for company. While he waited, he destroyed any incriminating evidence that linked Adam to himself, Olivia or Belle. Then, in the very early morning, he dragged Adam's body along the beach to the huge pipe that led under the promenade directly into the sea.

Will leant into the pipe; a stink of decaying rubbish was coming up from the tunnel. After the heavy rain, water gushed through it in a churned-up morass. Turgid earthy brown water. Dragging the corpse behind him, Will crawled into the pipe. The cold stinking water ran over his feet up to his knees. He lay the body carefully down on the ground, water pouring over the corpse, Adam's dark hair pulled towards the sea by the force of the current.

Chapter 28

Will drove up the long driveway to the private hospital through the landscaped gardens covered in late spring snow. The hospital was set in the suburbs of Edinburgh where meandering streets and bungalows formed a pattern only visible from above. The hospital was a postmodern building constructed from glass and metal and looked more like an art gallery than a place of healing.

A receptionist looked up grimly at Will as he walked through the automatic sliding doors into the hall. She was sitting behind a stainless steel desk that glimmered in the neon light like the coral gloss on her lips. Her hair was pulled back in a tight, clinical bun. The hospital seemed eerily empty. He felt that he and the receptionist were the only people in the building.

'I've come for some information about a girl.'

She smiled, revealing surprisingly wonky teeth.

'You don't look the type.'

He showed her his card.

'I'm a private investigator.' He was in no mood for repartee.

'Well, if that's the case, Private Investigator …' She didn't disguise her sarcasm.

'Do you have a record of Emily Blake? She may have been taken here a few years ago as an emergency case. With head injuries, I've been told. I don't have an exact date.'

She looked at him with his pale face, his dark curly hair, and his scruffy demeanour.

'Of course you don't.'

There was something in her sardonic manner and the mocking look in her green eyes that reminded him of someone.

'Rose!' he exclaimed.

She looked startled. For a moment she tried to seem as if she didn't know what he was talking about.

'Rose … moonlighting as a hospital receptionist. That's not a very respectable job for a hardworking prostitute.'

She looked furtively around the reception hall. 'Please keep your voice down.'

He smiled. 'I'll keep my voice down. If you tell me what I want to know.'

'It's highly confidential information. I'll get into trouble.'

He leant over. This time he whispered. 'I could get you into trouble, too.'

She shrugged her shoulders. 'Tell them. I don't care. They pay badly here, anyway.'

'If you do this for me, it might help find Jade.'

'It better,' Rose finally said, grumpily. She went into a back room and walked over to an incongruously old-fashioned filing cabinet and pulled open the bottom drawer to reveal a cuff of brown paper envelopes.

'Here we are… No, no record of an Emily Blake,' she called out to him through the open door.

'What about a Louise Verver?'

She kept flicking, 'Verver. Yes, here we are. L Verver.'

She returned to her desk with the file.

'She was in a car accident,' Will said. He remembered Adam Verver telling him he had met Louise in the hospital, while he was doing research into memory.

She shook her head. 'No mention of a car accident. A head injury.'

Too many coincidences. It was Emily who was supposed to have suffered a head injury.

'Louise suffered severe trauma to the brain,' Rose continued, as she read from the file. 'When her father brought her in, she was delirious. Perhaps you've got the two girls muddled up.'

'Delirious?'

'She kept repeating the same words over and over again. The doctor noted them down: *"The poor bird. The cat on the wall is going to eat it. Tell the girl in the painting. The cat is going to eat it."* Unfortunately, she went on to suffer severe memory loss.'

'There are no records of her address?'

'No. But we do have her father's address – Dr Adam Verver, Flat 2, The Promenade.'

'Adam Verver is not her father,' Will said quietly. He then turned and fled out of the reception into the snow.

'Don't mention it,' shouted Rose as the glass doors slid noiselessly shut behind him.

~

The manager of the amusement arcade looked up at him.

'I expect you've come for her.'

'So you've known all along.'

'The arcade is owned by his father. So Adam has full run

of the place.'

'But the father doesn't know?'

'Lord Verver has a vague suspicion, perhaps. No more than that. But he is fiercely protective of his son. Always has been.'

'And you did nothing?'

'Adam looked after her well. She was tucked away in the basement, but within walking distance from his flat. But now that he's apparently disappeared – so the newspapers say – there will be no one to look after her.'

Will felt he was in a nightmare in which everyone wore the masks of everyday normality, masks which hid disfigured monsters who had no idea what they really looked like. They themselves believed in the masks. After all, he believed in his. He wanted to rip the masks off and show them their real faces in the mirror. But not now.

'Give me the key.'

'He never did her any harm. He was like a father to her.'

'I'm her father,' William said quietly, taking the key from his hand. The manager gave him a strange look. 'I am her father and he had no right to take her away from me and now I've got her back.'

Will went down the stairs he had gone down before to the basement. He could hear faint music coming from behind a large stack of boxes. He pulled the boxes down to reveal a hidden door. The original recording of *Mister Sandman* was coming from the other side. He unlocked the door and opened it. Belle's daughter ran into his open arms and just for a second it didn't matter to him that she wasn't Emily.

~

As Will walked down the promenade it occurred to him that Portobello was the residue of everything. Not only the residue of a successful Victorian resort with a zoo and ladies of leisure holidaying with their servants in the Georgian cottages, the residue of a wealthy heyday, but also a place full of accumulated memories. He fitted in well. For he was living the residue of his life. The passion of his youth had left him, leaving him with this wonderful carcass of small daily pleasures. He was left with the deserted beach and the empty plastic bottles on the shore and the odd straggling stranger on the promenade walking his dog. He was safe and Portobello kept him safe. He could solve his cases, and walk away unharmed.

He was resigned to the belief that Adam had murdered Emily. Now called Louise, she had run away from him, and Adam must have found her again and killed her. He had continued to keep Will on the case, enjoying the fact that Will was looking for his own daughter without realizing it. Where her body was, he had no idea. Emily had disappeared again forever. Whether she had ever remembered he was her father, he had no idea. He remained, he thought triumphantly, in all ways untouchable.

~

The singer packed her bags in the dressing room of Granny's Attic. She didn't have many clothes, only the ones she had bought since she had run away. One day she was sure she would remember everything but at the moment there were only the dark and light strands of her past. Memories shifting over her mind like wind shifting over the sand.

THE FALCONER
(ISBN 9781906120238; £8.99)

It is 1936. Iris Tennant applies to become personal assistant to Lord Melfort, the Under-Secretary of War, at his private estate in the Scottish Highlands. Her secret plan is to find out why her younger sister Daphne committed suicide there a year previously. As Iris gradually falls under the spell of Glen Almain, she starts to see the apparition of Daphne haunting its glades and begins to wonder about the manner of her death. Is there really a beast that inhabits the woods? Who is the mysterious falconer? What actually happened to Daphne, and is Iris destined for the same fate? A backdrop of impending war and the spectre of Nazi Germany lom over this strange, dark tale. What ensues is a battle between instinct and reason, fantasy and history. Award-winning writer Alice Thompson's compelling new novel is a story of transformation; an exploration of the shifting borderlands between imagination and reality.

'There's folk and fairy tale in this, some whimsy, some Angela Carter-style sensuality, combined with an earthy realism, and a thriller-style plot... Thompson's writing is, as ever, the kind that demands full attention – important details are embedded in lyrical description or insinuated into an apparently innocuous observation. This is not a book that is kind to readers – you have to buy into the world its author has created, accept its own very special laws – and that requires effort. But it's effort that is ultimately rewarded: I doubt you'll read another book quite like it this year.' *The Scotsman*

'The world she creates is claustrophobic and hypnotic, recognisably a dream but also rational on its own, admittedly skewed, terms... Many novelists bore readers to sleep. Wake up to *The Falconer*.' *The Sunday Herald*

Two Ravens Press is the most northerly literary publisher in the UK, operating from a six-acre working croft on a sea-loch in the north-west Highlands of Scotland. Two Ravens Press is run by two writers with a passion for language and for books that are non-formulaic and that take risks. We publish cutting-edge and innovative contemporary fiction, non-fiction and poetry.

Visit our website for comprehensive information on all of our books and authors – and for much more:

- browse all Two Ravens Press books (print books and e-books) by category or by author, and purchase them online at a discount on retail price, post & packing-free (in the UK, and for a small fee overseas)

- there is a separate page for each book, including summaries, extracts and reviews, and author interviews, biographies and photographs

- read our regular blog about life as a small literary publisher in the middle of nowhere – or the centre of the universe, depending on your perspective – with a few anecdotes about life down on the croft thrown in.

www.tworavenspress.com